A Soldier's Play

A DRAMA

by Charles Fuller

Winner of the 1982
PULITZER PRIZE FOR DRAMA

S A M U E L   F R E N C H ,   I N C .
25 WEST 45TH STREET   NEW YORK 10036
7623 SUNSET BOULEVARD   HOLLYWOOD 90046
LONDON   *TORONTO*

MUSIC INFORMATION

You may cause new music to be composed for use with the author's lyrics in connection with your performances of the play or if you wish, SAMUEL FRENCH, INC. can supply you with an instrumental score for harmonica and guitar, for a period of eight weeks, on receipt of the following:

1. Number of performances & exact performance dates.
2. A $10.00 blanket music rental fee.
3. Music royalty.
   A. $3.00 per amateur performance
   B. $20.00 per week (or part thereof) for stock performances
4. $25.00 refundable deposit, which is returned upon the safe delivery of the material to Samuel French, Inc.

If you request special handling, special delivery, UPS or air mail, you will be billed for the excess postage.

THEATRE FOUR
424 West 55th Street
(Near Ninth Avenue)
246-8545

the Negro Ensemble Company

DOUGLAS TURNER WARD
Artistic Director

LEON B. DENMARK
Managing Director

presents
A SOLDIER'S PLAY

by
CHARLES FULLER

with

CHARLES BROWN	JAMES PICKENS, JR.
SAMUEL L. JACKSON	DENZEL WASHINGTON
EUGENE LEE	PETER FRIEDMAN
COTTER SMITH	STEVEN A. JONES
ADOLPH CAESAR	LARRY RILEY
BRENT JENNINGS	STEPHEN ZETTLER

Directed by
DOUGLAS TURNER WARD

Scenery by	*Costumes by*
FELIX E. COCHREN	JUDY DEARING
Lighting by	*Sound by*
ALLEN LEE HUGHES	REGGE LIFE

Production Stage Manager
CLINTON TURNER DAVIS

4

Premier Performance — November 10, 1981

WARNING

CAST
(*in order of appearance*)

Tech/Sergeant Vernon C. Waters . . . . . ADOLPH CAESAR
Captain Charles Taylor . . . . PETER FRIEDMAN
Corporal Bernard Cobb . . . . EUGENE LEE
Private First Class Melvin
    Peterson. DENZEL WASHINGTON
Corporal Ellis. . . . . JAMES PICKENS, JR.
Private Louis Henson . . . . SAMUEL L. JACKSON
Private James Wilkie . . . . STEVEN A. JONES
Private Tony Smalls . . . . BRENT JENNINGS
Captain Richard Davenport . . . . CHARLES BROWN
Private C. J. Memphis . . . . LARRY RILEY
Lieutenant Byrd . . . . COTTER SMITH
Captain Wilcox . . . . STEVEN ZETTLER

Time: 1944 Place: Ft. Neal, Louisiana

THERE WILL BE A 15-MINUTE INTERMISSION

The photographing or sound recording of any portion
of this production ... reproduced upon the stage or ...

CAST

(in order of appearance)

...	...

Place: ... Orleans, Louisiana

For LARRY NEAL
whom I will miss
for the rest of my life.

A Soldier's Play

ACT ONE

TIME: *1944*

PLACE: *Fort Neal, Louisiana*

SCENE: *The inner shell of the stage is black. On the stage, in a horseshoe like half-circle are several platforms at varying levels.*

On the S.R. *side of this horseshoe is a military office arrangement with a small desk, two office type chairs, straight-backed, a regimental and American flag. A picture of F.D.R. is on the wall.*

On the S.L. *side of the horseshoe, and curved toward the rear is a barracks arrangement, with three bunk beds and footlockers set in typical military fashion. The exit to this barracks is a doorway on the Far Left. (This barracks should be changeable—these bunks with little movement can look like a different place.) On the edge of this barracks is a poster, semi-blown up of Joe Louis in an Army uniform, helmet, rifle and bayonet. It reads: PVT. JOE LOUIS SAYS, "WE'RE GOING TO DO OUR PART—AND WE'LL WIN BECAUSE WE'RE ON GOD'S SIDE."*

On the rear of the horseshoe U.C. *is a bare platform, raised several feet above everything else, it can be anything we want it to be—a limbo if you will.*

The entire set should resemble a courtroom. The sets, barracks and office, will both be elevated, so that from anywhere on the horseshoe one may look

*down onto a space at c.s. that is on the stage floor.
The levels should have easy access either by stairs or
ramps, and the entire set should be raked ever so
slightly so that one does not perceive much difference between floor and set, and the bottom edges of
the horseshoe. There must also be enough area on
both sides of the horseshoe to see exits and en-
trances.*

*Lighting will play an integral part in the realization of
the play. It should therefore be sharp, so that areas
are clearly defined, with as little spill into other
areas as possible. Lights must also be capable of
suggesting mood, time and place.*

*As the play opens, the stage is black. In the background
rising in volume we hear a popular song of the
1940's.* Quite suddenly, in a sharp though nar-
row beam of light, in limbo, TECH-SERGEANT
VERNON C. WATERS, a well-built light brown-
skinned man in a World War II, winter Army
uniform, is seen down on all fours. He is stinking
drunk, trying to stand and mumbling to himself, as
the MUSIC FADES.*

WATERS. (*repeating*) They still hate you! They still
hate you . . . They still hate you! (*WATERS is
laughing as suddenly SOMEONE steps into the light.
[We never see this person.] He is holding a .45 caliber*

---

*In the New York production the author suggested "Don't Sit Under
the Apple Tree," by the Andrews Sisters. This is a copyrighted song,
written by Lew Brown, Sam Stept and Charles Tobias and, if it is
desired to use the same song in any subsequent productions of A
Soldier's Play, each producer must individually obtain permission in
writing from: Robbins Music, c/o United Artists, 6754 Hollywood
Blvd, Los Angeles CA 90028

pistol. He lifts it swiftly and ominously toward Waters'
head and fires. WATERS is knocked over backward.
He is dead. There is a strong silence onstage.)

VOICE. Les' go!

(*The MAN with the gun takes a step, then stops. He*
points the gun at WATERS again and fires a second
time. There is another silence as limbo is plunged
into darkness and the popular song of the 1940's is
heard in the distance.

As the LIGHTS RISE, we are in the barracks of Com-
pany B, 221st Chemical Smoke Generating Com-
pany, at Fort Neal. FIVE BLACK ENLISTED
MEN stand at "parade rest" with their hands above
their heads and submit to a search. They are COR-
PORAL BERNARD COBB, a man in his mid to
late 20's, dressed in a T-shirt, dog tags, fatigues,
and combat boots. PRIVATE JAMES WILKIE, a
man in his early 40's, a career soldier. He is dressed
in fatigues from which his stripes have been re-
moved, a baseball cap and is smoking a cigar.
PRIVATE LOUIS HENSON, thin in his late 20's,
early 30's. He is wearing a baseball T-shirt that
reads: Ft. Neal on the front, and #4 on the back,
fatigues, and boots. PRIVATE FIRST CLASS
MELVIN PETERSON, a man in his late 20's. He
wears glasses, T-shirt. He looks angelic. He does
not look sloppy. Of all the MEN, his stripe is the
most visible, his boots the most highly polished.
PRIVATE TONY SMALLS, a man in his late 30's,
a career man. He is as his name feels. All five men
are being searched by CORPORAL ELLIS, a
soldier who is simply always "spit and polish."
ELLIS is also black and moves from man to man

*patting them down in a police-like search. CAP-
TAIN CHARLES TAYLOR, a young white man in
his mid to late 30's, looks on a bit disturbed. All the
men's uniforms are from World War II.*
WILKIE, PETERSON, SMALLS, COBB, and HEN-
SON *stand on Level A facing front, with their
hands on their heads. ELLIS frisks PETERSON,
finishes, then crosses* s.l. *to SMALLS. He frisks
him, finishes and then crosses to COBB and HEN-
SON, frisking both men respectively. TAYLOR
stands* d.c. *facing* u.s. *addressing the men.*)

TAYLOR. I'm afraid this kind of thing can't be helped
men — you can put your arms down when Ellis finishes.
(*WILKIE and PETERSON put their hands down and
stand at ease. As ELLIS finishes each man, they stand at
ease.*) We don't want anyone from Fort Neal going into
Tynin looking for red-necks. (*He crosses* s.r., *pacing.*)

COBB. May I speak, Sir? (*TAYLOR nods.*) Why do
this, Captain? They got M.P.'s surrounding us, and
hell, the Colonel must know nobody colored killed the
man!

TAYLOR. This is a precaution, Cobb. We can't have
revenge killings, so we search for weapons.

PETERSON. Where'd they find the Sarge, Sir?

TAYLOR. (*pacing* d.s. *crossing* s.r. *to* s.l.) In the
woods out by the Junction — and so we don't have any
rumors. Sergeant Waters was shot twice — we don't
know that he was lynched! (*pause*) Twice. Once in the
chest, and a bullet in the head. (*ELLIS finishes frisking
HENSON and stands at ease* d.s. *of* s.l. *platform.*) You
finished the footlockers?

ELLIS. (*stands at attention*) Yes, Sir! There aren't any
weapons.

TAYLOR. (*relaxing*) I didn't think there would be. At ease, men! (*The MEN relax.*) Tech-Sergeant Waters, in my opinion, served the 221st and this platoon in particular with distinction, and I for one shall miss the man. (*Slight pause. TAYLOR continues to pace* D.S.C.) But no matter what we think of the Sergeant's death, we will not allow this incident to make us forget our responsibility to this uniform. We are soldiers, and our war is with the Nazis and Japs, not the civilians in Tynin. Any enlisted man found with unauthorized weapons will be immediately subject to Summary Court Martial. (*crosses* S.R.; *softens*) Sergeant Waters' replacement won't be assigned for several weeks. Until that time you will all report to Sergeant Dorsey of C Company—any questions? (*crosses* D.S.C.) Corporal Cobb will be barracks N.C.O.

PETERSON. Who do they think did it, Sir?

TAYLOR. (*crosses* US.) At this time there are no suspects.

HENSON. You know the Klan did it, Sir.

TAYLOR. Were you an eyewitness, Soldier?

HENSON. Who else goes around killin' Negroes in the South? — They lynched Jefferson the week I got here, Sir! And that Signal Corps guy, Daniels, two months later!

TAYLOR. Henson, (*He crosses to HENSON; HENSON comes to attention.*) unless you saw it, keep your opinions to yourself! Is that clear? (*HENSON nods.*) And that's an order! It also applies to everybody else!

ALL. (*almost simultaneously*) Yes, Sir! (*HENSON stands at ease.*)

TAYLOR. (*crossing* D.C. *to face* U.S.) You men who have details this afternoon, report to the Orderly room for your assignments. The rest of you are assigned to the

Colonel's quarters—clean up detail. Cobb, (*COBB stands at attention.*) I want to see you in my office at 1350 hours.

COBB. Yes, Sir. (*He stands at ease.*)

TAYLOR. As of 0600 hours this morning, the town of Tynin was placed off-limits to all military personnel. (*slight groan from the MEN*) The Friday night dance has also been cancelled—(*All the MEN moan, TAYLOR is sympathetic.*) OK, OK! Some of the Officers are going to the Colonel—I can't promise anything. Right now, it's cancelled. (*He looks at ELLIS.*)

ELLIS. Ten-hutt! (*The MEN snap-to, the CAPTAIN salutes, COBB only salutes him back. The CAPTAIN starts out.*)

TAYLOR. As you were!

(*The CAPTAIN and ELLIS exit the barracks* S.L. *The MEN move to their bunks or footlockers. WILKIE crosses* D.S.L.; *looks out window. SMALLS crosses to* U.R.C. *Box, sits. PETERSON crosses to* U.C. *Box and sits. COBB crosses to* S.L., *looks out over COBB'S shoulder; then paces* S.L. *platform. SMALLS crosses to* S.R.C. *Box, sits.*)

COBB. They still out there, Wilkie?

WILKIE. Yeah. (*He crosses to* D.R.C. *window, looks out. Takes small cigar out of his shirt pocket.*) Got the whole place surrounded.

HENSON. I don't know what the hell they thought we'd go into that town with—mops and dishrags?

WILKIE. Y'all "recruits" know what Colonel's-clean-up-detail is don't you? (*He crosses to* S.L. *bunk and sits; takes out a deck of cards.*) Shovelin' horseshit in his stables—

COBB. Ain't no different from what we been doin'. (*He begins scratching around his groin area.*)

PETERSON. (*crossing* S.L. *to COBB*) Made you the barracks Commander-in-Chief, huh? (*COBB nods.*) Don't git like ole Stone-ass—What are you doin'?

COBB. Scratchin'!

(*HENSON crosses to* S.L. *bunk and takes green fatigue shirt and hat out of bunk. Places them on top of the bunk. He takes off his baseball shirt.*)

HENSON. (*overlapping*) Taylor knows the Klan did it—I hope y'all know that!

SMALLS. (*suddenly*) Then why are the MP's outside with rifles? Why hold us prisoner? (*He rises, crosses to* C.S. *on level A.*)

PETERSON. They scared we may kill a couple "peckerwoods," Smalls. Calm down, man!

(*SMALLS crosses* S.R., *sits* S.R.C. *Box. WILKIE begins to shuffle the cards.*)

WILKIE. (*quickly*) Smalls, you wanna' play some Coon-can? (*SMALLS shakes his head, "no". He is quiet, staring.*)

COBB. (*examining himself*) Peterson, you know I think Eva gave me the "crabs."

(*PETERSON rises and crosses to* U.C. *Box. HENSON, putting on his fatigue shirt, crosses* U.C. *to COBB.*)

HENSON. Cobb, the kinda' women you find, it's a wonda' your nuts ain't fell off—crabs? You probably got lice, ticks, bed-bugs, fleas—tapeworms—

COBB. Shut up, Henson! Pete—I ain't foolin', Man!

PETERSON. Get some powder from the PX.

WILKIE. (*almost simultaneously*) Which one of y'all feels like playin' me some cards? (*He looks at HENSON.*)

HENSON. Me and Peterson's goin' down the messhall—(*crosses* S.R. *to PETERSON*) you still goin', Pete?

PETERSON. (*nodding*) Wilkie? I thought all you could do was play, "Go-fer"? (*He opens* U.C. *box and takes out shirt and cap and puts on shirt.*)

HENSON. (*slyly*) Yeah, Wilkie—whose ass can you kiss, now that your number one ass is dead?

COBB. (*laughing*) That sounds like something C.J. would sing! (*looks at himself again*) Ain't this a bitch? (*picks at himself*)

WILKIE. (*overlapping to HENSON*) You know what you can do for me, Henson. (*HENSON gives PETERSON a dirty gesture.*) You too, Peterson!

PETERSON. Naughty, naughty!

WILKIE. I'm the one lost three stripes—and I'm the only man in here with kids, so when the man said, jump, I jumped!

HENSON. (*derisively*) Don't put your wife and kids between you and Waters' ass, man!

WILKIE. I wanted my stripes back!

COBB. I'm goin' to sick-call after chow.

WILKIE. (*continuing*) Y'all ain't neva' had nothin', that's why you can't understand a man like me! There was a time I was a Sergeant Major, you know! (*HENSON waves disdainfully at him turning his attention to COBB.*)

HENSON. Ole' V-girl slipped Cobb the crabs! How you gonna' explain that to the girl back home, Corporal? How will that fine, big-thighed Moma feel, when the only ribbon you bring home from this war is the Purple Heart for crab bites? (*He laughs.*)

SMALLS. (*rising*) Don't any of you guys give a damn?

PETERSON. What's the matta', Smalls?

SMALLS. The man's dead! We saw him alive last night!

COBB. (*quickly*) I saw him too. At least I know he died good and drunk!

SMALLS. (*loudly*) What's the matter with y'all?

HENSON. The man got hisself lynched! We're in the South, and we can't do a goddamn thing about it—you heard the Captain! But don't start actin' like we guilty of somethin'. (*softens*) I just hope we get lucky enough to get shipped outta' this hell hole to the War! (*He crosses to* S.L. *bench and picks up fatigue hat and puts it on. To himself:*) Besides, whoever did it, didn't kill much anyway.

SMALLS. He deserved better than that!

(*COBB rises, fastens pants, opens box and takes out fatigue shirt.*)

COBB. Look, everybody feels rotten, Smalls. But it won't bring the man back, so let's forget about it!

(*PETERSON moves to pat SMALLS on the back.*)

PETERSON. Why don't you walk it off, man?

(*SMALLS moves away to his bunk. PETERSON shrugs. HENSON crosses to* S.L. *box, picks up baseball shirt and folds it.*)

HENSON. Yeah—or go turn on a smoke machine, let the fog make you think you in London!

(*SMALLS sits down on his bunk and looks at them for a moment, then lays down.*)

WILKIE. (*overlapping*) Let Cobb bring his Eva over. (*He rises.*) She'll take his mind off Waters plus give him a bonus of crabs! (*He crosses above* S.L. *box and exits. The MEN laugh, but SMALLS doesn't move as the lights begin to slowly fade out.*)

HENSON. (*counting*)—an blue-balls. Clap. Syphilis. Pimples! (*He crosses* S.L. *above* L. *box, to exit.*)

(*PETERSON crosses* S.L., *following HENSON out. COBB exits* S.L., *following PETERSON; jokingly he tosses his shirt at HENSON as he exits. SMALLS lays down on* S.R.C. *box.*)

HENSON. (*continued, as he exits*) Piles! Fever blisters. Cock-eyes. Cooties!

(*The MEN are laughing as the lights go out. A solo harmonica is heard in the background. In the BLACKOUT, SMALLS exits* U.R. *CAPTAIN DAVENPORT enters* S.L., *crosses to* D.L. *corner of Level A. As a special rises on him we see a rather wiry Black Officer carrying glasses, dressed sharply in an MP uniform, his hat cocked to the side and "strapped" down the way the airmen wear theirs, he is carrying a briefcase. We are aware of a man who is very confident and self-assured. He is smiling as he faces the audience. The solo harmonica begins to fade as DAVENPORT begins to speak.*)

DAVENPORT. Call me Davenport—Captain, United States Army, attached to the 343rd military Police Corps Unit, Fort Neal, Lousiana. (*A slow blues har-*

monica plays faintly in background under monologue.)
I'm a lawyer the segregated Armed Services couldn't find
a place for. My job in this war? Policing colored troops.
(*crosses* D.L.C. *into another Special; slight pause*) One
morning, during mid-April, 1944, a colored Tech-
Sergeant, Vernon C. Waters, assigned to the 221st
Chemical Smoke Generating Company, stationed here,
before transfer to Europe, was brutally shot to death in
a wooded section off the New Post Road and the junction of Highway 51 — just two hundred yards from the
colored N.C.O. club, by a person or persons unknown.
(*crosses* D.C.; *pauses a little*) Naturally, the unofficial
concensus was the local Ku Klux Klan, and for that
reason, I was told at the time, Colonel Barton Nivens
ordered the Military Police to surround the enlisted
men's quarters — then instructed all his Company Com-
manders to initiate a thorough search of all personal
property for unauthorized knives, guns — weapons of
any kind. (*slight pause*) You see, ninety percent of the
Colonel's command — all of the enlisted men stationed
here are Negroes, and the Colonel felt (*He crosses* S.L.
into first Special.)

(*ELLIS enters* D.R., *crosses up Ramp to table preset*
U.R. *He picks up the table, turns around and places
it on* S.R. *Platform, lights in this area rise dimly. He
crosses down* S.R. *Ramp to 2 stacked chairs* S.R. *he
picks up chairs and crosses up Ramp. He places
chairs under* S.R. *side of table, and the other under*
S.L. *side of table. All of ELLIS' blocking is continuous with DAVENPORT'S monologue.*)

DAVENPORT. (*continued*) and I suppose justly, that
once word of the Sergeant's death spread among his
troops, there might be some retaliation against the white

citizens of Tynin. (*He shrugs and crosses* D.L.C.) What he did worked—there was no retaliation, and no racial incidents. (*Pause*) The week after the killing took place, several correspondents from the Negro press wrote lead articles about it. But the headlines faded—(*He crosses* D.R.C. *into another special.*)

(*ELLIS crosses* S.L. *on level A to* C. *Boxes. He picks up larger unit and crosses* D.C. *Places Box on spike marks. ELLIS crosses to* U.L.C. *and picks up smaller Box; crosses to* C. *and places* L. *of larger unit. He then crosses to smaller unit* U.C., *picks up, and places* C. *to right of larger unit. Smiles.*)

DAVENPORT. (*continued*) The NAACP got me involved in this. Rumor has it, Thurgood Marshall ordered an immediate investigation of the killing, and the Army, pressured by Secretary of War Stimson, rather randomly ordered Colonel Nivens to initiate a preliminary inquiry into the Sergeant's death. Now, the Colonel didn't want to re-hash the murder, but he compiled with the Army's order by instructing the Provost Marshal, my C.O. Major Hines, to conduct a few question and answer sessions among the men of Sergeant Waters' platoon and file a report. The matter was to be given the lowest priority.

(*CAPTAIN TAYLOR, carrying an army personnel file, enters* S.R., *crosses up Ramp and* D.S. *into office area. He stands* S.L. *of* L. *Chair, reading papers from folder. ELLIS crosses* U.S. *to limbo platform, crosses* S.R., *down ramp and exits.*)

DAVENPORT. (*continued, pause. He puts on sunglasses.*) The case was mine, five minutes later. It was four to five weeks after his death—(*He picks up brief-case.*) the month of May. (*Crosses* u.s., *stands* s.r. *of* r. *Chair. The lights fade over rest of stage; the harmonica fades out. He pauses as the light builds in CAPTAIN TAYLOR's office. TAYLOR is facing DAVENPORT, expressionless. DAVENPORT is a bit puzzled.*) Captain?

TAYLOR. Forgive me for occasionally staring, Davenport, you're the first colored officer I've ever met. I'd heard you had arrived a month ago. You're a bit startling. (*quickly*) I mean you no offense. (*starts back to his desk and sits on the edge of it, as DAVENPORT starts into the office a bit cautiously*) We'll be getting some of you as replacements, but we don't expect them until next month. Sit down, Davenport. (*DAVENPORT sits and places briefcase on the table. TAYLOR reads papers in file.*) You came out of Fort Benning in '43?

DAVENPORT. Yes.

TAYLOR. And they assigned a lawyer to the Military Police? I'm infantry and I've been with the Engineers, Field Artillery and Signal Corps—this is some Army. Where'd you graduate Law School?

DAVENPORT. Howard University.

TAYLOR. Your daddy a rich minister or something? (*DAVENPORT shakes his head "no".*) I graduated the Point—(*He places file on table, rises. Pause.*) We didn't have any Negroes at the Point. I never saw a Negro until I was twelve or thirteen. (*pause*) You like the Army I suppose, huh?

DAVENPORT. Captain, did you see my orders?

TAYLOR. (*bristling slightly*) I saw them right after Colonel Nivens sent them to Major Hines. I sent my Orderly to the barracks and told him to have the men waiting for you.

DAVENPORT. Thank you.

TAYLOR. I didn't know at the time that Major Hines was assigning a Negro, Davenport. (*DAVENPORT stiffens.*) My preparations were made in the belief that you'd be a white man. I think it only fair to tell you, that had I known what Hines intended I would have requested the immediate suspension of the investigation—may I speak freely?

DAVENPORT. You haven't stopped yet, Captain.

TAYLOR. Look—how far could you get even if you succeed? These local people aren't going to charge a white man in this parish on the strength of an investigation conducted by a Negro!—and Nivens and Hines know that! The Colonel doesn't give a damn about finding the men responsible for this thing! And they're making a fool of you—can't you see that?—and—take off those sunglasses!

DAVENPORT. I intend to carry out my orders—and I like these glasses—they're like MacArthur's.

TAYLOR. You go near that Sheriff's office in Tynin in your uniform—carrying a briefcase, looking and sounding white and charging local people and you'll be found just as dead as Sergeant Waters! People around here don't respect the Colored!

DAVENPORT. I know that.

TAYLOR. (*annoyed*) You know how many times I've asked Nivens to look into this killing? Every day, since it happened, Davenport. Major Hines didn't tell you that!

DAVENPORT. Do you suspect someone, Captain?

TAYLOR. Don't play cat and mouse with me, Soldier! (*He crosses* S.L.)

DAVENPORT. (*calmly*) Captain, like it or not, I'm all you've got. I've been ordered to look into Sergeant

Water's death, and I intend to do exactly that. (*There is a long pause.*)

TAYLOR. Can I tell you a little story? (*DAVENPORT nods.*) Before you were assigned here? Nivens got us together after dinner one night, and all we did was discuss Negroes in the officer ranks. (*crosses to* S.L. *chair, pulls it out*) We all commanded Negro troops, but nobody had ever come face to face with colored officers—there were a lot of questions that night—for example, your quarters—had to be equal to ours, but we had none—no mess-hall for you! (*slight pause; crosses to* S.L. *chair, pulls it out*) Anyway, Jed Harris was the only officer who defended it—my own feelings were mixed. The only Negroes I've ever known were subordinates—My father hired the first Negro I ever saw—man named Colfax, to help him fix the shed one summer—Nice man—worked hard—did a good job too. (*remembering; smiles, thoughtfully*) But I never met a Negro with any education until I graduated the Point—hardly an officer of equal rank. So I frankly wasn't sure how I'd feel—until right now—and—(*struggling; leans against chair*) I don't want to offend you, but I just can not get used to it—the bars, the uniform—being in charge just doesn't look right on Negroes!

DAVENPORT. Captain, are you through?

TAYLOR. (*leans over table to DAVENPORT*) You could ask Hines for another assignment—this case is not for you! By the time you overcome the obstacles to your race this case would be dead!

DAVENPORT. (*sharply*) I got it. And I *am* in charge! All your orders instruct you to do is cooperate! (*There is a moment of silence.*)

TAYLOR. I won't be made a fool of, Davenport.

(*straightening*) Ellis! (*to DAVENPORT:*) You're right, there's no need to discuss this any further.

(*ELLIS enters* DS.R. *and crosses up the ramp. He crosses* U.L. *of the table, salutes and stands at attention.*)

ELLIS. Yes, Sir!

TAYLOR. Captain Davenport will need assistance with the men—I can't prevent that, Davenport, but I intend to do all I can to have this so-called "investigation" stopped.

DAVENPORT. Do what you like. (*He rises; pushes chair under table; picks up briefcase.*) If there's nothing else, you'll excuse me won't you, Captain?

TAYLOR. (*sardonically*) Glad I met you, Captain. (*DAVENPORT salutes and TAYLOR returns it. For an instant the TWO MEN trade cold stares. TAYLOR picks up the file folder crosses* DS.R. *and exits* S.R. *DAVENPORT removes his glasses.*)

(*ELLIS steps down into the office area; stands below* S.R.C. *Box.*)

ELLIS. We heard it was you, Sir—you know how the grapevine is. Sad thing—what happened to the Sarge.

DAVENPORT. What's on the grapevine about the killing?

ELLIS. We figure the Klan. They ain't crazy about us tan yanks in this part of the country.

(*ELLIS and DAVENPORT cross* S.L. *on Level A to* S.L. *platform. ELLIS puts on his cap. The lights fade in the office and rise* S.L. *and* D.C. *in the interrogation area.*)

DAVENPORT. Is there anything on the grapevine about trouble in the town before Sergeant Waters was killed?

ELLIS. None that I know of before — after, there were rumors around the Post — couple of our guys from the Tank Corps wanted to drive them "Shermans" into Tynin — then I guess you heard that somebody said two officers did it — I figure that's why the Colonel surrounded our barracks.

DAVENPORT. Was the rumor confirmed — I didn't hear that! Did anything ever come of it?

ELLIS. Not that I know of, Sir.

DAVENPORT. Thanks, Ellis — I'd better start seeing the men. (*ELLIS gestures toward the interrogation area.*) Did you set this up? (*ELLIS nods and crosses to* s.l. *of the boxes. DAVENPORT crosses into* c. *area; stands* s.r. *of* R. *box.*) Good — (*He sets his briefcase on the table.*) Are they ready?

ELLIS. The Captain instructed everybody in the Sarge's platoon to be here, Sir. He told them you'd be starting this morning. (*DAVENPORT smiles.*)

DAVENPORT. (*to himself:*) Before he found out, huh? (*sits*)

ELLIS. (*puzzled*) Sir?

DAVENPORT. Nothing. Call the first man in, Corporal — and stay loose, I might need you.

ELLIS. Yes, Sir! (*He salutes. DAVENPORT returns it. ELLIS takes a step back, about face, takes a step and turns.*) Sir, May I say something? (*DAVENPORT nods. ELLIS crosses* s.r. *toward DAVENPORT.*) It sure is good to see one of us wearin' them Captain's bars, Sir.

DAVENPORT. Thank you. (*ELLIS salutes, does a sharp "about-face" and crosses to extreme* D.L.)

ELLIS. (*loudly*) Private Wilkie!

WILKIE. (*offstage*) Yes, Sir! (*Almost immediately*

WILKIE appears in the doorway, s.l. *He is dressed in proper uniform of fatigues, boots and cap.*)

ELLIS. Capn' wants to see you! (*WILKIE crosses* u.s. *of* s.l. *bunk; stands. ELLIS gestures for WILKIE to cross* d.c.)

WILKIE. Yes indeedy! (*Moves quickly to* d.c. *where he comes to "attention" and salutes. ELLIS crosses* r., *stands behind WILKIE.*) Private James Wilkie reporting as ordered, Sir.

DAVENPORT. At ease, Private. Have a seat. (*to ELLIS as WILKIE sits:*) That will be all, Corporal.

ELLIS. Yes, Sir. (*He salutes and does a sharp about face. He exits* s.l., *crossing below platforms. DAVENPORT waits until he leaves before speaking.*)

DAVENPORT. Private Wilkie, I am Captain Davenport—

WILKIE. (*interjecting*) Everybody knows that, Sir. You all we got down here. (*smiling broadly*) I was on that first detail got your quarters togetha', Sir. (*DAVENPORT nods.*)

DAVENPORT. (*coldly*) I'm conducting an investigation into the events surrounding Sergeant Waters' death. Everything you say to me will go in my report, but that report is confidential.

WILKIE. I understand, Sir. (*DAVENPORT removes pad and pencil from the briefcase.*)

DAVENPORT. How long did you know Sergeant Waters?

WILKIE. 'Bout a year, Sir. I met him last March—March 5th—I remember the date, I had been a Staff Sergeant exactly two years the day after he was assigned. This company was basically a baseball team then, Sir. See, most of the boys had played for the Negro League, so naturally, the Army put us all together. (*chuckles at the memory*) We'd be assigned to different companies—Motor Pool—Dump Truck all week long—made us do the dirty work on the Post—garbage, clean-up—but on Saturdays we were whippin' the hell out of 'em on the baseball diamond! I was hittin' .352 myself! And we had a boy, C.J. Memphis? He coulda' hit a ball from Fort Neal to Berlin, Germany—or Tokyo—if he was battin' right-handed. (*pauses, catches DAVENPORT's impatience*) Well, the Army sent Waters to manage the team. He had been in Field Artillery—Gunnery Sergeant. Had a Croix De Guerre from the First War too.

DAVENPORT. What kind of man was he?

WILKIE. All spit and polish, Sir.

(*At that moment in limbo a spotlight hits SERGEANT WATERS. He is dressed in a well-creased uniform, wearing a helmet-liner and standing at "parade-rest" facing the audience. The light around him however is strange—it is blue-grey like the past. The light around DAVENPORT and WILKIE abates somewhat. Dialogue is continuous.*)

DAVENPORT. Tell me about him.

WILKIE. He took my stripes! (*smiling*) But I was in the wrong, Sir!

(*WATERS stands at ease. His voice is crisp and sharp. His movements minimal. He is the typical hard nosed NCO—strict, soldierly.*)

WATERS. Sergeant Wilkie! (*WILKIE sits at attention. DAVENPORT focuses on WILKIE.*) You are a non-commissioned officer in the Army of a country at war—the penalty for being drunk on duty is severe in peace-time, so don't bring me no po'-colored-folks-can't-do-nothin'-unless-they-drunk-shit as an excuse! You are supposed to be an example to your men—so, I'm gonna' send you to jail for 10 days *and* take them goddamn stripes. Teach you a lesson—you in the Army! (*derisively*) Colored folks always runnin' off at the mouth 'bout what y'all gonna' do, if the white man gives you a chance—and you get it, and what do you do with it? You wind up drunk on guard duty—I don't blame the white man—why the hell should he put colored and white together in this war? You can't even be trusted to guard your own quarters—no wonder they treat us like dogs—Get outta' my sight, *Private!*

(*Light fades at once on WATERS, who then exits* u.l.)

DAVENPORT. What about the other men?

WILKIE. Sometimes the Southern guys caught a little hell—Sarge always said he was from up North somewhere. He was a good soldier, Sir. I'm from Detroit myself—born and raised there. Joe Louis started in Detroit—did you know that, Sir?

DAVENPORT. What about the Southerners?

WILKIE. Sarge wasn't exactly crazy 'bout 'em—'cept for C.J. (*A few bars of solo harmonica are heard offstage. C.J. MEMPHIS, a young, handsome black man in a soldier's uniform, enters* s.l., *playing harmonica and carrying a guitar. He crosses onto platform above* s.l. *Box. He sits on the onstage side of Box and then begins to play guitar. The light is the strange light of the past.*)

C.J. (*singing, his voice deep, melodious and bluesy*)

It's a low/ it's a low, low/ lowdown dirty shame! Yeah, it's a low/ it's a low, low/ lowdown dirty shame!

WILKIE. (*before C.J. finishes*) Big, Mississippi boy! (*WILKIE and C.J. simultaneously sing.*)

C.J. & WILKIE. They say we fightin' Hitler! But they won't let us in the game! (*C.J. strums and hums.*)

WILKIE. Worked harder and faster than everybody—wasn' a man on the team didn't like him. Sarge took to him the first time he saw him. "Wilkie," he says,

(*WATERS enters* U.L. *dressed in khaki uniform. He crosses to* U.L.C. *locker, props foot on it and snaps fingers in time to music.*)

WILKIE & WATERS. (*simultaneously*) What have we got here?

WATERS. A guitar playin' man! Boy, you eva' heard of Blind Willie Reynolds? Son House? Henry Sims? (*C.J. nods to everything.*)

C.J. You heard them play, Sarge?

WATERS. Everyone of 'em. I was stationed in Mississippi couple years ago—you from down that way, ain't you?

C.J. Yes, Sah! (*WATERS crosses to C.J.*)

WATERS. Well they useta' play over at the Bandana Club outside Camp J.J. Reilly.

C.J. I played there once!

WATERS. (*smiling*) Ain't that somethin'? I'd go over there from time to time—People useta' come from everywhere! (*to WILKIE:*) Place was always dark, Wilkie—smoky. Folks would be dancin'—sweatin'—guitar pickers be strummin', shoutin'— it would be wild in there sometimes. Reminded me of a place I useta' go

in France durin' the First War— the women, the whis-
key—place called the Cafe Napoleon.

C.J. You really like the Blues, huh?

WATERS. No other kind of music—where'd you learn
to play so good? I came by here yesterday and heard this
"pickin"—one of the men tol' me it was you.

C.J. My Daddy taught me, Sarge.

WATERS. You play pretty good, boy. Wilkie, wasn'
that good?

(*WATERS exits* U.L. *C.J. rises playing guitar, crosses
above* S.L. *bunk and exits* S.L. *His playing fades in
background as the lights fade* S.L.)

WILKIE. Yes indeed, Sarge. (*to DAVENPORT:*) I
mostly agreed with the Sarge, Sir. (*DAVENPORT rises,
crosses* D.L.) He was a good man. Good to his men.
Talked about his wife and kids all the time—Useta'
write home every day. I don't see why nobody would
want to kill the Sarge, Sir.

(*WATERS enters* U.L., *in khaki uniform without tunic,
smoking a pipe. He crosses* D.R. *on "limbo" platform, as lights rise in this area.*)

WATERS. Wilkie? (*WILKIE rises, focuses front,
listening to WATERS.*) You know what I'ma get that
boy of mine for his birthday? One of them Schwinn
bikes. He'll be 12—time flies don't it? Let me show you
something?

WILKIE. (*to DAVENPORT*) He was always pullin'
out snapshots, Sir. (*He crosses* U.S.C. *and stands below*
R.C. *Box as the lights dim in the interrogation area and a*

Special focuses on DAVENPORT. WATERS hands WILKIE a snapshot.)

WATERS. My wife let a neighbor take this a couple weeks ago — ain't he growin' fast?

WILKIE. He's over your wife's shoulder! (*Hands it back, WATERS looks at the photo.*)

WATERS. I hope this kid never has to be a soldier.

WILKIE. It was good enough for you.

WATERS. I couldn't do any better — and this Army was the closest I figured the white man would let me get to any kind of authority. No, the Army ain't for this boy. When this war's over, things are going to change, Wilkie — and I want him to be ready for it — my daughter too! I'm sendin' both of 'em to some big white college — (*puts photo in wallet and replaces it in his pocket*) Let 'em rub elbows with the whites, learn the white man's language — how he does things. Otherwise we'll be left behind — you can see it in the Army. White man runnin' rings around us.

WILKIE. (*sitting on the R.C. bunk*) A lot of us didn't get the chance or the schoolin' the white folks got.

WATERS. That ain't no excuse, Wilkie. Most niggahs just don't care — tomorrow don't mean nothin' to 'em. My Daddy shoveled coal from the back of a wagon all his life. He couldn't read or write, but he saw to it we did! Not havin' ain't no excuse for not gettin'.

WILKIE. Can't get pee from a rock, Sarge. (*WATERS crosses S.L. on limbo platform.*)

WATERS. You just like the rest of 'em, Wilkie — I thought bustin' you would teach you something — we got to challenge this man in his arena — use his weapons, don't you know that? We need lawyers, doctors — Generals — Senators! Stop thinkin' like a Niggah!

WILKIE. All I said—

WATERS. Is the equipment ready for tomorrow's game?

WILKIE. Yeah.

WATERS. Good. You can go now, Wilkie. (*WILKIE is stunned.*)

WATERS. That's an order!

(*WATERS exits* U.L. *WILKIE rises, crosses* D.L. *to DAVENPORT. The lights fade out in the limbo area and rise in the interrogation area.*)

WILKIE. He could be two people sometimes, Sir. Warm one minute—Ice the next.

DAVENPORT. How did you feel about him?

WILKIE. Overall—I guess he was alright. You could always borrow a ten spot off him if you needed it.

DAVENPORT. (*crossing* S.R.) Did you see the Sergeant anytime immediately preceding his death?

WATERS. (*sitting* S.L. *on the* S.L. *Box*) I don't know how much before it was, but a couple of us had been over the NCO Club that night and Sarge had been juicin' pretty heavy.

DAVENPORT. Did Waters drink a lot? (*He sits; makes notes on pad.*)

WILKIE. No more than most—(*pause*) Could I ask you a question, Sir? (*DAVENPORT nods.*) Is it true, when they found Sarge all his stripes and insignia were still on his uniform?

DAVENPORT. I don't recall it being mentioned in my preliminary report. Why?

WILKIE. If that's the way they found him, something's wrong ain't it, Sir? Them Klan boys don't like to see us in these uniforms. They usually take the stripes and stuff off, before they lynch us. (*DAVENPORT is quiet, thoughtful for a moment.*)

DAVENPORT. Thank you, Private—I might want to call you again, but for now, you're excused. (*WILKIE rises.*)

WILKIE. Yes, Sir! (*WILKIE salutes, takes step back, about faces. Sudden mood swing, hesitant.*) Sir?

DAVENPORT. Yes?

WILKIE. (*crossing to DAVENPORT*) Can you do anything about allotment checks? My wife didn' get hers last month.

DAVENPORT. There's nothing I can do directly—did you see the finance officer? (*WILKIE nods.*) Well—I'll—I'll mention it to Captain Taylor.

WILKIE. Thank you, Sir. You want me to send the next man in?

(*DAVENPORT nods. WILKIE salutes, does an "about-face" and exits S.L. DAVENPORT returns the salute then leans back in his chair thoughtfully. In the background, the harmonica of C.J. rises again as the next man, P.F.C. MELVIN PETERSON enters, crosses above the S.L. Box and D.L.C. to DAVENPORT. Dressed in fatigues, he is the model soldier. He walks quickly to the table, stands at attention and salutes. The harmonica fades out as DAVENPORT returns the salute.*)

PETERSON. Private First Class Melvin Peterson reporting as ordered, Sir!

DAVENPORT. Sit down, Private. (*PETERSON sits and removes his cap.*) Do you know why I'm here?

PETERSON. Yes, Sir.

DAVENPORT. Fine. Now, everything you tell me is confidential, so I want you to speak as freely as possible. (*PETERSON nods.*) Where are you from?

PETERSON. Hollywood, California—by way of Alabama, Sir. I enlisted in '42—I thought we'd get a chance to fight.

DAVENPORT. (*ignoring the comment*) Did you know Sergeant Waters well?

PETERSON. No, Sir. He was already with the Company when I got assigned here. And us common G.I.'s don't mix well with NCO's.

DAVENPORT. Were you on the baseball team?

PETERSON. Yes, Sir—I played shortstop.

DAVENPORT. Did you like the Sergeant?

PETERSON. No, Sir.

(*Before DAVENPORT can speak, ELLIS enters S.L., crosses above the S.L. Box and D.S.L. to the S.R. corner of the S.L. platform, level A.*)

ELLIS. Beg your pardon, Sir. Captain Taylor would like to see you in his office at once.

DAVENPORT. Did he say why?

ELLIS. No, Sir—just that you should report to him immediately.

DAVENPORT. (*annoyed*) Tell the men to stick around. When I finish with the Captain I'll be back.

ELLIS. Yes, Sir! (*ELLIS salutes. DAVENPORT returns it. ELLIS executes right face; exits S.L.*)

DAVENPORT. (*to PETERSON:*) Feel like walking, Private? We can continue this on the way. (*beginning to put his things in his briefcase*) Why didn't you like the Sergeant?

PETERSON. It goes back to the team, Sir. I got here in
—baseball season had started so it had to be June—
June of last year. The team had won maybe 9–10 games
in a row, there was a rumor that they would even get a
chance to play the Yankees in exhibition. So when I got
assigned to a team like that, Sir—I mean I felt good.
Anyway, ole' Stone-ass—

DAVENPORT. Stone-ass?

PETERSON. I'm the only one called him that—Sergeant
Waters, Sir.

DAVENPORT. Respect his rank, with me, Private.

PETERSON. I didn't mean no offense, Sir. (*slight
pause*) Well, (*PETERSON and DAVENPORT rise.
DAVENPORT picks up his briefcase and sunglasses.*)
the Sergeant and that brown-nosin' Wilkie? (*DAVEN-
PORT stops, turns and looks at PETERSON reprov-
ingly.*) They ran the team—and like it was a chain-gang,
Sir. A chain-gang!

(*The two men exit S.L. As they do C.J. MEMPHIS,
HENSON, COBB and SMALLS enter in their
baseball uniforms. Shirts with Fort Neal stamped
on the fronts and numbers on the back and baseball
caps. They are carrying equipment—bats, gloves.
C.J. is carrying his guitar. SMALLS enters tossing
a baseball into the air and catching it. They almost
all enter at once with the exuberance of young men.
Their talk is locker-room loud, and filled with
bursts of laughter as the lights change.*)

HENSON. (*crossing to U.L.C. foot locker; miming
pitching baseball.*) You see the look on that umpire's
face when C.J. hit that home run? I thought he was
gonna' die on the spot, he turned so pale!

(*C.J. crosses to* D.L.C. *Box in interrogation area, places Box in top of show preset position. Sits. COBB crosses to* U.L. *Box and sits; opens the box and takes out boots and shoe brush. They move to their respective bunks.*)

SMALLS. Serves the fat bastard right! Some of them pitches he called strikes were well ova' my head! (*He crosses* S.R. *to* R.C. *Box. Places glove and ball on top of box, crosses to* D.R.C. *Box, places Box* U.C. *in top of show preset position, then crosses to* D.C. *Box. Picks it up and places it in top of show preset position. C.J. strums his guitar, COBB begins to brush off his boots.*)

COBB. C.J.? Who was that fine, river-hip thing you was talkin' to, "Homey"? (*C.J. shrugs and smiles.*)

HENSON. (*crossing to* S.L. *bunk and placing glove and ball; crosses to* U.L.C. *Box; stands to* R. *of COBB.*) Speakin' of women, I got to write my Lady a letter. (*He begins to dig for his writing things.*)

COBB. She looked mighty good to me, C.J.

SMALLS. (*overlapping*) Y'all hear Henson? Henson you ain't had a woman since a woman had you! (*HENSON makes an obscene gesture.*)

C.J. (*overlapping SMALLS*) Now all she did was ask me for my autograph.

COBB. Look like she was askin' you fo' mor'n that. (*to SMALLS:*) You see him, Smalls? Leanin' against the fence, all in the woman's face, breathin' heavy—

HENSON. If Smalls couldn't see enough to catch a ground ball right in his glove, how the hell could he see C.J. ova' by the fence?

SMALLS. (*crossing* S.L. *to HENSON*) That ball got caught in the sun!

HENSON. (*miming fielding and fumbling a ground ball; sits*) On the ground?

COBB. (*at once*) We beat 'em nine to one! (*SMALLS crosses to* S.R.C. *Box, opens it and places baseball glove and ball inside.*) Y'all be quiet, I'm askin' this man 'bout a woman he was with had tits like two helmets!

C.J. If I hada' give that gal what she asked fo'—she'da give me somethin' I didn' want! Them V-gals git you a bad case a' clap. 'Sides she wasn' but 16.

SMALLS. You shoulda' introduced her to Henson—16's about his speed. (*He crosses to* R.C. *Box. He sits; takes off his baseball shoes and massages his feet. HENSON makes a farting sound in retaliation. Opens* U.L.C. *Box; takes out letter, envelope, pencil and paper.*)

C.J. Aroun' home? There's a fella' folks useta' call, Li'l Jimmy One Leg—on account of his thing was so big? Two years ago—ole young pretty thing laid clap on Jimmy so bad, he los' the one good leg he had! Now, folks jes' call him little! (*All laugh.*) That young thing talkin' to me ain' look so clean.

HENSON. Dirty or clean, she had them white boys lookin'.

COBB. Eyes poppin' out they sockets, wasn' they? Remind me of that pitcher las' week! The one from 35th Ordnance? The one everybody claimed was so good? Afta' 12 straight hits, he looked the same way!

(*PETERSON enters* S.L. *carrying 4 baseball bats in an equipment bag. He crosses above* S.L. *Box to* C. *bunk, places equipment bag inside and sits on Box.*)

SMALLS. It might be funny ta' y'all but when me and Pete had duty in the Ordnance Mess-hall, that same white pitcher was the first one started the name callin'. (*He rises and opens the* U.R.C. *Box; places shoes inside.*)

HENSON. Forget them Dudes in Ordnance—lissen to

this! (*He begins to read from a short letter.*) Dear,
Louis—y'all hear that? The name is Louis—

COBB. Read the damn letter!

(*SMALLS takes off shirt and sits on the* R.C. *Box.*)

HENSON. (*making an obscene gesture*) Dear, Louis.
You and the boys keep up the good work. All of us here
at home are praying for you and inspired in this great
cause by you. We know the Nazis and the Japs can't be
stopped unless we all work together, so tell your buddies
to press forward and win this war. All our hopes for the
future go with you, Louis, Love Mattie. I think I'm in
love with the Sepia Winston Churchill—what kinda' letter do you write a nut like this?

COBB. Send her a round of ammunition and a
bayonet, *Louis!* (*HENSON waves disdainfully.*)

PETERSON. (*laying down on bunk*) Y'all oughta' listen
to what Smalls said. Every time we beat them at
baseball, they get back at us every way they can.

COBB. It's worth it to me just to wipe those superior
smiles off they faces.

PETERSON. I don't know—seems like it makes it that
much harder for us.

C.J. They tell me, coupla' them big-time Negroes is
on the verge a' gittin' all of us togetha'—colored and
white—say they want one Army.

PETERSON. Forget that, C.J.! White folks'll neva' in-
tegrate no Army!

C.J. (*strumming*) If they do—I'ma be ready for 'em!
(*He stands, props foot on Box; sings and plays.*) Well, I
got me a bright red zoot-suit / And a pair a' patent
leatha' shoes / And my woman she sittin' waitin' / Fo'
the day we hea' the news! Lawd, lawd, (*The other men*

join C.J. singing, keeping time with the music by beating the sides of their bunks, laughing, etc. PETER-SON sits up.) lawd, lawd, / Lawd, lawd, lawd, lawd!

(*SERGEANT WATERS, followed by WILKIE, enters* s.l., *immediately crossing to the* c. *of the barracks, his strident voice cutting off C.J.'s singing and playing abruptly. WILKIE stands* s.l.)

WATERS. Listen up! (*to C.J.:*) We don't need that guitar playin'-sittin'-round-the-shack music today, C.J.! (*smiling*) I want all you men out of those baseball uniforms and into work clothes! You will all report to me at 1300 hours in front of the Officers Club. We've got a work detail. We're painting the lobby of the club. (*collective groan*)

SMALLS. The Officers can't paint their own club?

COBB. Hell no, Smalls! Let the great-colored-clean-up-company do it! Our motto is: Anything you don't want to do, the colored troops will do for you!

HENSON. (*rising; like a cheer:*) Anything you don't want to do, the colored troops will do for you! (*He starts to lead the OTHERS.*)

OTHERS. Anything you don't want to do, the colored troops will do for you!

WATERS. That's enough! (*The MEN are instantly silent.*)

HENSON. When do we get a rest? We just played nine innings of baseball, Sarge!

SMALLS. (*standing and crossing to* u.r.c.) We can't go in the place, why the hell should we paint it?

COBB. (*rising and placing shoes and brush inside* u.l.c. *Box*) Amen, brother! (*He sits.*)

(*There is a moment of quiet before WATERS speaks.*)

WATERS. Let me tell you fancy-assed ball-playin' Negroes somethin'! The *reasons* for any orders given by a Superior Officer is none of y'all's business! You obey them! This country is at war, and you niggahs are soldiers—nothin' else! So baseball teams—win or lose, get no special privileges! They need to work some of you niggahs till your legs fall off!

(*SMALLS and HENSON exchange looks of disgust. SMALLS crosses* s.r. *below* r.c. *Box.*)

WATERS. (*continued; intensely*) And something else: (*He crosses to SMALLS.*)—from now on when I tell you to do something, I want it done—is that clear? (*The MEN are quiet.*) Now, Wilkie's gonna' take all them funky shirts you got on over to the laundry. (*WILKIE crosses to C.J.; gestures to him to take off shirt; SMALLS tosses his shirt to WILKIE.*) I could smell you suckers before I hit the field! (*He crosses* D.R.)

PETERSON. What kinda' colored man are you?

(*WATERS stops immediately; turns to PETERSON.*)

WATERS. I'm a soldier, Peterson! First, last and always! I'm the kinda' colored man that don't like lazy, shiftless Negroes!

PETERSON. You ain't got to come in here and call us names!

WATERS. The Nazis call you "schvatza"! You gonna' tell them they hurt your little feelings?

C.J. Don't look like to me we could do too much to them Nazis wit' paint brushes, Sarge. (*The MEN laugh. The moment is gone and though WATERS is angry, his tone becomes overly solicitous, smiling.*)

WATERS. (*crossing to C.J.*) You tryin' to mock me, C.J.?

C.J. No sah, Sarge.

WATERS. Good, because whatever an ignorant, low-class geechy like you has to say, isn't worth paying attention to, is it? (*pause*) Is it?

C.J. I reckon not, Sarge.

(*WATERS crosses* D.R.)

PETERSON. You a creep, Waters!

WATERS. (*turning to PETERSON*) Boy, you are something — ain't been in the company a month, Wilkie, and already everybody's champion!

C.J. (*interjecting*) Sarge was just jokin', Pete — He don't mean no harm!

PETERSON. He does! (*He rises, takes off baseball shirt; tosses it to WILKIE. He then opens Box, throws his baseball cap inside.*) We take enough from the white boys!

WATERS. Yes you do (*He crosses* L.C.) — and if it wasn' for you Southern niggahs, yessahin', bowin' and scrapin', scratchin' your heads, white folks wouldn' think we were all fools!

PETERSON. Where you from, England? (*He crosses* S.R. *on Level A. Men snicker.*)

HENSON. (*immediately*) Peterson! (*rises*)

WATERS. (*immediately*) You got somethin' to say, Henson? (*crossing* U.L.C. *to HENSON*)

HENSON. Nothin', Sarge. (*He shakes his head as WATERS turns back to PETERSON.*)

WATERS. Peterson, you got a real comic streak in you. Wilkie, looks like we got us a wise-ass Alabama boy here! (*He moves toward PETERSON.*) Yes, sir — (*He snatches PETERSON in the collar.*) Don't get smart, Niggah!

PETERSON. Get your fuckin' hands off me! (*He pushes WATERS' hand away; WATERS stumbles.*)

WATERS. (*smiling and leaning forward*) You wanna' hit ole Sergeant Waters, boy? (*whispering*) Come on! (*He assumes a stance ready to fight.*) Please! (*He places his hands behind his back and juts his chin towards PETERSON.*) Come on, Niggah!

(*CAPTAIN TAYLOR enters the barracks from* s.l. *quite suddenly unaware of what is going on and crosses* d.l.)

HENSON. Tenn-Hut! (*All the men snap-to.*)

(*WATERS stands* d.r. *opposite TAYLOR; SMALLS stands below* r.c. *Box. PETERSON stands* r.c. *on Level A; HENSON stands below* u.l.c. *Box; COBB stands below* u.l. *bunk; C.J. stands below* l.c. *Box; WILKIE stands* s.l. *on Level A.*)

TAYLOR. At ease! (*He moves toward WATERS feeling the tension.*) What's going on here, Sergeant?

WATERS. Nothin', Sir—I was going over the Manual of Arms—Is there something in particular you wanted, Sir? Something I can do?

TAYLOR. (*relaxing somewhat*) Nothing—(*to the men:*) Men, I congratulate you on the game you won today. We've only got seven more to play, and if we win them, we'll be the first team in Fort Neal history to play the Yanks in exhibition. Everyone in the Regiment is counting on you. (*pats C.J. on shoulder*) In times like these morale is important—and winning can help a lot of things. (*pause*) Sergeant, as far as I'm concerned, they've got the rest of the day off. (*He crosses* D.S.L. *as if to exit. The men are pleased.*)

WATERS. (*crossing* S.L. *to TAYLOR*) Begging your pardon, Sir, (*TAYLOR stops, turns to face WATERS.*) but these men need all the work they can get. They don't need time off — our fellas' aren't getting time off in North Africa — besides we've got orders to report to the Officers Club for a paint detail at 1300 hours.

TAYLOR. Who issued that order?

WATERS. Major Harris, Sir.

TAYLOR. I'll speak to the Major. (*He turns to exit.*)

WATERS. Sir! (*He steps* S.L. *TAYLOR stops, turns and faces WATERS.*) I don't think it's such a good idea to get a colored NCO mixed up in the middle of you officers, Sir.

TAYLOR. I said, I'd speak to him, Sergeant.

WATERS. Yes, Sir!

TAYLOR. I respect the men's duty to service, but they need time off.

WATERS. Yes, Sir. (*He salutes, does an about face and crosses* D.R. *Pause.*)

TAYLOR. You men played a great game of baseball out there today — that catch you made in centerfield, Memphis — how the hell'd you get up so high?

C.J. (*shrugging and smiling*) They say I got "Bird" in mah' blood, Sir.

(*TAYLOR is startled by the statement, his smile is an uncomfortable one. WATERS is standing on "eggs".*)

TAYLOR. American eagle I hope. (*He laughs a little.*)
C.J. No, Sah', Crow — (*WATERS starts to move but*

C.J. *stops him by continuing—several of the men are beginning to get uncomfortable.*) Man tol' my Daddy the day I was born, the shadow of a crow's wings—

TAYLOR. (*cutting him off*) Fine—Men, I'll say it again—you played superbly. (*turning to WATERS*) Sergeant. (*He starts out abruptly.*)

WATERS. Tenn-hut! (*He salutes as the MEN snap-to.*)

TAYLOR. (*exiting*) As you were. (*TAYLOR salutes as he exits stage left.*)

(*There is an instant of quiet. The men relax a little, but their focus is C.J., who stands and crosses to PETERSON. HENSON crosses to S.L. bunk, sits, and unties his shoes.*)

WATERS. (*laughing*) Ain't these geechies somethin'? How long a story was you gonna' tell the man, C.J.? My God! (*The men join in laughing, but as he turns toward PETERSON he stiffens.*) Peterson! Oh, I didn't forget you, Boy. (*The room quiets.*) It's time to teach you a lesson!

PETERSON. Why don't you drop dead, Sarge?

(*SMALLS sits on the S.R. Box. HENSON crosses to PETERSON. They sit on the U.C. Box. COBB crosses to C.J. and whispers to him. C.J. sits on the L.C. Box. WILKIE stands on the S.L. platform.*)

WATERS. Nooo! I'ma drop you, boy! Out behind the barracks—Wilkie, you go out and make sure it's all set up.

WILKIE. You want all the NCO's? (*WATERS nods. WILKIE exits S.L., smiling.*)

WATERS. (*crossing S.L. onto the S.L. platform, then*

crossing U.S. *and standing above C.J.*) I'm going out-side and wait for you, geechy! And when you come out, I'm gonna' whip your black Southern ass — let the whole company watch it too! (*pointing*) You need to learn respect, boy — how to talk to your betters. (*HENSON crosses* L. *and sits* U.L.C. *on the footlocker. WILKIE crosses* S.R. *to WATERS. WATERS takes off his hat and gives it to WILKIE.*) Fight hard, hea'? I'ma try to bust your fuckin' head open — the rest of you get those goddamn shirts off like I said! (*He exits. The barracks is quiet for a moment.*)

(*COBB stands and takes off his shirt.*)

COBB. You gonna' fight him?
HENSON. (*overlapping*) I tried to warn you!
PETERSON. You ain't do nothin'! (*HENSON places pencil, pad, letter and envelopes in* U.L.C. *Box.*)
SMALLS. He'll fight you dirty, Pete — don't do it!
COBB. You don't want to do it?
PETERSON. You wanna' fight in my place, Cobb? (*He sits.*) Shit!

(*Slight pause, HENSON pulls off his shirt.*)

C.J. (*COBB crosses* S.L. *to HENSON. They look off* S.L.) I got some "Farmers Dust" — jes' a pinch'll make you strong as a bull — they say it comes from the city of Zar. (*removes a pouch from his neck*) I seen a man use this stuff and pull a full grown mule outta a sink hole by hisself! (*SMALLS crosses to COBB and HENSON.*)
PETERSON. Get the hell outta' here, with that back-water, crap — can't you speak up for yourself — let that bastard treat you like a dog!

C.J. 'Long as his han's ain't on me—he ain't done me no harm, Pete. Callin' names ain't nothin', I know what I is. (*softening*) Sarge ain't so bad—been good to me.

PETERSON. The man despises you!

C.J. Sarge? You wrong, Pete—plus I feel kinda' sorry for him myself. Any man ain't sure where he belongs, must be in a whole lotta' pain.

PETERSON. Don't y'all care?

HENSON. Don't nobody like it, Pete—but when you here a little longer—I mean, what can you do? This hea's the Army and Sarge got all the stripes.

(*PETERSON rises disgusted and crosses* S.L. *SMALLS rises and croses* S.L.)

SMALLS. Peterson, look, if you want me to, I'll get the Captain. You don't have to go out there and get your head beat in!

PETERSON. Somebody's got to fight him. (*He exits. There is quiet as SMALLS walks back to his bunk.*)

C.J. (*singing*)

It's a low / it's a low, low / lowdown
   dirty shame!
It's a low, low, low / lowdown dirty shame!
Been playin' in this hea' Army / an ain't even learned
   the game! Lawd, lawd, lawd, lawd—

(*C.J. begins to hum as the lights slowly fade out over the barracks. As they do, the lights come up simultaneously in the CAPTAIN's office. It is empty. PETERSON [in proper uniform] and DAVENPORT enter from* S.R. *They stop outside the CAPTAIN's office.*)

PETERSON. He beat me pretty bad that day, Sir. The man was crazy!

DAVENPORT. Was the incident ever reported?

PETERSON. I never reported it, Sir—I know I should have, but he left me alone after that. (*He shrugs.*) I just played ball.

DAVENPORT. Did you see Waters the night he died?

PETERSON. No, Sir—me and Smalls had guard duty.

DAVENPORT. Thank you, Private. That'll be all for now. (*PETERSON comes to attention.*)

DAVENPORT. By the way, did the team ever get to play the Yankees?

PETERSON. No, Sir. We lost the last game to a Sanitation Company. (*He salutes. DAVENPORT returns it. PETERSON does a crisp right face, crosses U.S. and exits U.R. Slowly DAVENPORT starts into the CAPTAIN's office surprised that no-one is about.*)

DAVENPORT. Captain?

(*There is no response. For a moment or two DAVENPORT looks around. He is somewhat annoyed. He places his briefcase on the desk, and stands behind the S.R. chair. TAYLOR enters. He crosses to his desk where he sits in the S.L. chair and places a folder containing the memos on the desk.*)

TAYLOR. I asked you back here because I wanted you to see the request I've sent to Colonel Nivens to have your investigation terminated. (*He picks up several sheets of paper on his desk and hands them to DAVENPORT, who ignores them.*)

DAVENPORT. What?

TAYLOR. I wanted you to see that my reasons have

nothing to do with you personally — my request will not hurt your Army record in any way! — (*pause*) — there are other things to consider in this case!

DAVENPORT. Only the color of my skin, Captain.

TAYLOR. (*sharply*) I want the people responsible for killing one of my men found and jailed, Davenport!

DAVENPORT. So do I!

TAYLOR. Then give this up! (*He rises.*) Whites down here won't see their duty — or justice. They'll see *you!* And once they do, the Law — Due Process — it all goes! And what is the point of continuing an investigation that can't possibly get at the truth?

DAVENPORT. Captain, my orders are very specific, so unless you want charges brought against you for interfering in a criminal investigation, stay the hell out of my way and leave me, and my investigation, alone.

TAYLOR. (*almost sneering*) Don't take yourself too seriously, Davenport. You couldn't find an officer within five hundred miles who would convey charges to a Court Martial board against me, for something like that, and you know it! (*DAVENPORT crosses u.s. of table to TAYLOR.*)

DAVENPORT. Maybe not, but I'd — I'd see to it that your name, rank and duty station got into the Negro Press! Yeah, let a few colored newspapers call you a Negro-hater! Make you an embarrassment to the United States Army, Captain — like Major Albright at Fort Jefferson, and you'd never command troops again — or wear more than those Captain's bars on that uniform, Mr. West Point! (*TAYLOR rises.*)

TAYLOR. I'll never be more than a Captain, Davenport, because I won't let them get away with dismissing things like Waters death. I've been the Commanding Officer of three outfits! I raised hell in all of them, so threatening me won't change my request. Let the Negro press print that I don't like being made a fool of with phony investigations!

DAVENPORT. (*Crossing* S.R., *he studies TAYLOR for a moment.*) There are two white officers involved in this, Captain—aren't there?

TAYLOR. I want them in jail—out of the Army! And there is no way *you* can get them charged, or Court-Martialed or put away! The white officers on this post won't let you—they won't let me! (*He crosses* S.L.)

DAVENPORT. Why wasn't there any mention of them in your preliminary report? (*He sits on the* S.R. *chair.*) I checked my own summary on the way over here, Captain—nothing! You think I'ma let you get away with this? (*There is a long silence. TAYLOR walks back to his desk as DAVENPORT watches him. TAYLOR sits.*) Why?

TAYLOR. I couldn't prove the men in question had anything to do with it.

DAVENPORT. Why didn't you report it?

TAYLOR. I was ordered not to. (*pause*) Nivens and Hines. The doctors took two .45 caliber bullets out of Waters—Army issue. But remember what it was like that morning? If these men had thought a white officer killed Waters there would have been a slaughter! (*pause*) Cobb reported the incident innocently the night before—then suddenly it was all over the Fort.

DAVENPORT. Who were they, Captain? I want their names! (*DAVENPORT opens briefcase and takes out folder and pencil.*)

TAYLOR. Byrd and Wilcox. Byrd's in Ordnance—Wilcox's with the 12th Hospital Group. I was Captain of the Guard the night Waters was killed. (*He crosses to table.*) About 2100 hours, Cobb came into my office and told me he'd just seen Waters and two white officers fighting outside the colored NCO club. I called *your* office, and when I couldn't get two MP's, I started over myself to break it up. When I got there—no Waters, no officers. I checked the officers billet and found Byrd and Wilcox in bed. Several officers verified they'd come in around 2130. I then told Cobb to go back to the barracks and forget it.

DAVENPORT. What made you do that?

TAYLOR. At the time there was no reason to believe anything was wrong! Waters wasn't found until the following morning. I told the Colonel what had happened the previous night, and about the doctor's report, and I was told, since the situation at the Fort was potentially dangerous, to keep my mouth shut until it blew over. He agreed to let me question Byrd and Wilcox, but I've asked him for a follow-up investigation every day since it happened. (*There is a slight pause as he sits in* S.L. *chair.*) When I saw you, I exploded—it was like he was laughing at me.

DAVENPORT. Then you never believed the Klan was involved?

TAYLOR. No. Now can you see why this thing needs—someone else?

DAVENPORT. What did they tell you, Captain? Byrd and Wilcox?

TAYLOR. They're not going to let you charge those two men!

DAVENPORT. (*snaps*) Tell me what they told you! (*TAYLOR is quiet for a moment.*)

TAYLOR. They were coming off bivouac. (*He rises, crosses above the table and stands* U.S. *of DAVENPORT.*)

(*SGT. WATERS enters* U.S.R. *and staggers into the* D.C. *"limbo" area. He is dressed as we first saw him; he is drunk. Simultaneously LT. BYRD, a spit and polish soldier in his 20's and CAPT. WILCOX, a medical officer, enter* U.L. *and cross to the* C. *of the "limbo" area. Both are in full combat gear—pistols, belts, packs—and both are tired. The two men see WATERS. In the background is the faint hum of C.J.'s music, as the lights change to focus on the "limbo" platform.*)

TAYLOR. (*continued*) They saw him outside the Club.

WATERS. Well, if it ain't the white boys! (*He straightens and begins to march in a mock circle and then in their direction. He is mumbling, barely audibly: "One, two, three, four! Hup, hup, three, four! Hup, hup, three four!"*)

BYRD. (*crossing* D.R. *on limbo platform, his speech overlaps WATERS*) And it wasn't like we were looking for trouble, Captain—were we, Wilcox? (*WILCOX shakes his head "no," but he is astonished by WATERS' behavior and stares at him disbelieving.*)

WATERS. White boys! All starched and stiff! Wanted everybody to learn all that symphony shit! That's what you were saying in France (*He crosses* D.L. *on limbo platform.*) and you know, I listened to you? Am I all right now? Am I?

BYRD. (*crossing to WATERS*) Boy, you'd better straighten up and salute when you see an officer or you'll find yourself without those stripes! (*WATERS twists his cap on his head and thumbs his nose at BYRD; stumbles* D.R.) Will you look at this niggah? (*loudly*) come to attention, Sergeant! That's an order!

WATERS. No, Sah! I ain't straightenin' up for ya'll no more! I ain't doin' nothin' white folks say do, no more! (*WATERS drunkenly marches* S.L. *on limbo platform. He does a sloppy 'left face' and then marches* U.S. *singing:*)
No-more, no-more / no-more, no-more, noooo!
No-more, no-more / no-more, no-more, noooooo!

(*BYRD faces TAYLOR as WATERS continues to sing.*)

BYRD. (*overlapping*) Sir, I thought the man was crazy!
TAYLOR. And what did you think, Wilcox?

(*BYRD moves toward WATERS, and WATERS, still singing low, drunk and staggering, does an about face and marches* D.L. *WILCOX watches apprehensively.*)

WILCOX. (*at once*) He did appear to be intoxicated, Sir — out of his mind almost! (*He turns to BYRD.*) Byrd, listen — (*BYRD pushes WILCOX* U.S.R. *and crosses* S.L.)
DAVENPORT. (*suddenly*) Did they see anyone else in the area?
TAYLOR. No. (*to BYRD:*) I asked them what they did next.
BYRD. I told that Niggah to shut up!
WATERS. (*sharply*) No! (*He turns sharply, executing a 'last about' face from the preceding march. Change of mood.*) Followin' behind y'all? Look what it's done to me! — I hate myself!
BYRD. Don't blame us, boy! God made you black, not me! (*WILCOX crosses* D.S. *to WATERS.*)

WATERS. (*smiling*) My Daddy useta' say—

WILCOX. Sergeant, get hold of yourself! (*BYRD pushes WILCOX* U.L.)

WATERS. (*pointing*) Listen! (*BYRD steps toward him.*)

BYRD. I gave you an order, Niggah! (*WILCOX grabs BYRD, and stops him from advancing.*)

WATERS. (*beginning to cry*) My Daddy said, "Don't talk like dis'—talk like that!" "Don't live hea'—live there!" (*He crosses* D.L.; *BYRD counter crosses* D.R. *To them:*) I've killed for you! (*to himself; incredulous*) And nothin' changed!

(*BYRD pulls free of WILCOX and charges WATERS, as C.J.'s music punctuates the action of the scene.*)

BYRD. He needs to be taught a lesson! (*He shoves WATERS onto the ground where he begins to beat and kick the man, until he is forcibly restrained by WILCOX. WATERS moans.*)

WILCOX. Let him be! You'll kill the man! He's sick—leave him alone! (*BYRD pulls away. He is flush. WATERS tries to get up.*)

WATERS. Nothin' changed—See? And I've tried everything! Everything!

BYRD. I'm gonna' bust his black ass to Buck Private—I should blow his coward's head off! (*He lifts WATERS forcibly by the shoulders and shouts:*) There are good men killing for you, niggah! Gettin' their guts all blown to hell for you!

(*WATERS is pushed* U.S.R. *and off by BYRD as WILCOX follows trying to restrain him. The lights in the limbo area fade. A trace of C.J.'s music is left*

on the air. The lights then rise full in the CAP-
TAIN's office as the C.J. music fades.)

DAVENPORT. Did they "shove" Waters again?

TAYLOR. No. (*TAYLOR crosses to* s.l. *of table;*
stands behind chair.) But Byrd's got a history of scrapes
with Negroes. They told me they left Waters at
2110—and everyone in the Officer's billet verifies they
were both in by 2130. And neither man left—Byrd had
duty the next morning, and Wilcox was scheduled at the
hospital 0500 hours—both men reported for duty.

DAVENPORT. I don't believe it. (*places pencil and*
folder in briefcase)

TAYLOR. I couldn't shake their stories—(*He sits on*
the s.l. *chair.*)

DAVENPORT. That's nothing more than officers lying
to protect two of their own and you know it. (*He begins*
to fasten briefcase.) I'm going to arrest and charge both
of them, Captain—and you may consider yourself con-
fined to your quarters pending my charges against *you!*

TAYLOR. What charges?

DAVENPORT. It was *your* duty to go over Nivens' head
if you had to!

TAYLOR. Will you arrest Colonel Nivens too, Davenport? Because he's part of their alibi—he was there
when they came in—played poker—from 2100 to 0330
hours the following morning, the Colonel—your Major
Hines, "Shack" Callahan—Major Callahan, and Jed
Harris—and Jed wouldn't lie for either of them!

DAVENPORT. They're all lying!

TAYLOR. Prove it, hotshot. (*rises, places chair under*
table, crosses D.L. *of table*) I told you all I know, now
you go out and prove it!

DAVENPORT. I will, Captain! (*He rises.*) You can bet your sweet ass on that! I will!

(*DAVENPORT and TAYLOR stand staring at each other. In the background, the sound of the 1940's popular song from the start of the play comes up again and continues to play as the lights fade to black.*)

END OF ACT ONE

ACT TWO

SCENE: *As before.*

LIGHT RISES slowly D.S. *We hear a snippet of a popular song of the 1940's, as DAVENPORT addresses the audience. He is carrying a folder.*

DAVENPORT. During May of '44, the Allies were making final preparations for the invasion of Europe! Invasion! Even the sound of it made Negroes think we'd be in it — be swept into Europe in the waves of men and equipment — I know I felt it. (*thoughtfully*) We hadn't seen a lot of action except in North Africa — or Sicily. But the rumor in orderly rooms that spring was, pretty soon most of us would be in combat — somebody said Ike wanted to find out if the colored boys could fight — shiiit, we'd been fighting all along — right here, in these small southern towns — (*intense*) I don't have the authority to arrest a white *"private"* without a white officer present! (*slight pause*) Then I get a case like this? There was no way I wouldn't see this through to its end. (*smiles*) And after my first twenty-four hours, I wasn't doing too badly. I had two prime suspects — a motive, and opportunity! (*pause*) I went to Colonel Nivens and convinced him that word of Byrd and Wilcox involvement couldn't be kept a secret any longer. However, before anyone in the Press could accuse him of complicity — I would silence all suspicions by pursuing the investigation openly — on his orders — (*mimics himself*) "Yes, sir, Colonel, you can even send along a white officer — not Captain Taylor though — I think he's a little too close to the case, Sir." Colonel Nivens gave me per-

56

mission to question Byrd and Wilcox and having succeeded sooo easily, I decided to spend some time finding out more about Waters and Memphis. Somehow the real drama seemed to be there, and my curiosity wouldn't allow me to ignore it.

(*The lights rise in the barracks area as HENSON enters* s.l. *and crosses to the* r.c. *Box, executes a "left face" and salutes DAVENPORT, who returns the salute.*)

DAVENPORT. Sit down, Private. (*HENSON sits.*) Your name is Louis Henson, is that right? (*He crosses* u.l.c.)

HENSON. Yes, Sir.

DAVENPORT. (*crossing to* c.) Tell me what you know about Sergeant Waters and C.J. Memphis. (*HENSON looks at him strangely.*) Is there something wrong?

HENSON. No, Sir—I was just surprised you knew about it.

DAVENPORT. Why?

HENSON. You're an officer.

DAVENPORT. (*quickly*) And?

HENSON. (*hesitantly*) Well—Officers are up here, Sir—and us enlisted men—down here. (*slight pause*) C.J. and Waters—that was just between enlisted men, Sir. But I guess ain't nothin' a secret around colored folks—not that it was a secret. (*shrugs*) There ain't that much to tell—Sir. Sarge ain't like C.J. When I got to the Company in May of las' year, the first person I saw Sarge "chew-out" was C.J.! (*He is quiet.*)

DAVENPORT. Go on.

HENSON. (*with a pained expression*) Is that an order, Sir?

DAVENPORT. Does it have to be?

HENSON. I don't like tattle-talin', Sir—an' I don't mean no offense, but I ain't crazy 'bout talkin' to officers—colored or white.

DAVENPORT. It's an order, Henson! (*HENSON nods.*)

HENSON. C.J. wasn' movin' fast enough for *him*. (*DAVENPORT crosses* D.R.C.) Said C.J. didn' have enough *fire-under-his behind* out on the field.

DAVENPORT. You were on the team?

HENSON. Pitcher. (*Pause. DAVENPORT urges with a look.*) He jus' *stayed* on C.J. all the time—every little thing, it seemed like to me—then the shootin' went down, and C.J. caught all the hell.

DAVENPORT. What shooting?

HENSON. The shootin' at Williams Golden Palace, Sir—here, las' year! Happened last year—way before you got here. Toward the end of baseball season. (*DAVENPORT nods his recognition as he crosses* D.R.) The night it happened (*Gunshots are heard in the background.*) a whole lotta' gunshots went off near the barracks. I had gotten drunk over at the Enlisted Mens Club, so when I got to the barracks I just sat down in a stupor!

(*Shots are heard in the distance. They grow ever closer as the lights fade in the barracks except for a spotlight on HENSON and on DAVENPORT D.R. In the partial blackout, PETERSON and COBB enter* S.L. *and cross to the* S.L. *and* U.L. *Boxes respectively. They carry their combat boots and place them* D.S. *of their Boxes. C.J. and SMALLS enter* U.L. *and cross to the* U.C. *Box and the* L.C. *Box. They all are dressed in their underwear; boxer shorts, T-shirts and socks. They all lay on the boxes asleep. HENSON is seated staring at the ground. He looks up once as the gunshots go off, as he does someone—we cannot be sure who, sneaks into the barracks as the men begin to shift and awaken. This person puts something under C.J.'s bed and rushes out U.L. HENSON watches—surprised at first, rising, then disbelieving. He shakes his head, then sits back down as several men wake up.*)

COBB. What the hell's goin' on? Don't they know a man needs his sleep? (*He is quickly back to sleep.*)

SMALLS. (*simultaneously*) Huh? Who is it? (*looks around, then falls back to sleep*)

DAVENPORT. Are you sure you saw someone?

HENSON. Well—I saw something, Sir.

DAVENPORT. What did you do?

(*The shooting suddenly stops and the men settle down.*)

HENSON. I sat, Sir—I was juiced—(*shrugs*) The gunshots weren't any of my business—plus I wasn't sure what I had seen in the first place, then out of nowhere, Sergeant Waters, he came in.

(*WATERS enters the barracks suddenly, followed by WILKIE, as the lights rise. HENSON stands immediately, staggering a bit.*)

WATERS. Alright, alright! Everybody up! Wake them, Wilkie! (*WILKIE moves around the bunks shaking the men as WATERS crosses D.C.*)

WILKIE. Let's go! Up! Let's go, you guys! (*COBB*

shoves WILKIE's hand aside angrily as the others awaken slowly.)

WATERS. Un-ass them bunks! Tenn-hut! (*The men snap-to. PETERSON stands right of* S.L. *Box. COBB stands below* U.L. *Box; C.J. stands below* U.C. *Box; SMALLS crosses* D.S. *and stands left of C.J., he is the last one in place. WATERS moves menacingly toward him. WILKIE stands "at ease"* D.L.) There's been a shooting! One of ours bucked the line at Williams payphone and three soldiers are dead! Two colored and one white MP. (*paces*) Now the man who bucked the line, he killed the MP, and the white boys started shootin' everybody — that's how our two got shot. And this lowdown Niggah we lookin' for, got chased down here — and was almost caught, 'til somebody in these barracks started shootin' at the men chasin' him. So, we got us a vicious, murderin' piece of black trash in here somewhere — and a few people who helped him. If any of you are in this, I want you to step forward. (*No-one moves.*) All you baseball Niggahs are innocent, huh? Wilkie, make the search. (*PETERSON turns around as WILKIE begins to search inside PETERSON'S Box.*) Eyes front!

PETERSON. I don't want that creep in my stuff!

WATERS. You don't talk at "Attention!" (*WILKIE will search three bunks, COBB, SMALLS and HENSON respectively, along with footlockers. Under C.J.'s bed he will find what he is looking for.*) I almost hope it is some of you geechies — get rid of you southern niggahs! (*to WILKIE:*) Anything yet? (*He paces* D.S.)

WILKIE. Nawwww!

WATERS. Memphis, are you in this?

C.J. No, sah, Sarge.

WATERS. How many of you were out tonight? (*HEN-SON immediately raises his hand.*)

SMALLS. I was over at Williams around seven — got me some Lucky Strikes — I didn't try to call home, though.

COBB. I was there, this morning'!

WATERS. Didn't I say *tonight* — Uncle?

WILKIE. Got somethin'! (*WILKIE is holding up a .45 caliber automatic pistol, Army issue. Everyone's attention focuses on it. The men are surprised, puzzled.*)

WATERS. Where'd you find it? (*WILKIE taps C.J. on the shoulder. C.J. pulls away.*)

C.J. Naaaawww, man!

WATERS. C.J.? This yours? (*WATERS takes gun.*)

C.J. You know it ain't mine, Sarge!

WATERS. It's still warm — how come it's under your bunk?

C.J. Anybody coulda' put it thea', Sarge!

WATERS. Who? Or maybe this .45 crawled in through an open window — looked around the whole room — passed Cobb's bunk, and decided to snuggle up under yours? Must be Voodoo, right, boy? Or some of the Farmers Dust round that neck of yours, huh?

C.J. That pistol ain't mine!

WATERS. Liar!

C.J. No, Sarge — I hate guns! Makes me feel bad jes' to see a gun!

WATERS. You're under arrest (*He gives WILKIE the .45. WILKIE places .45 in his hip belt and takes C.J.'s arm.*) Wilkie, escort this man to the stockade! (*He crosses D.C.*)

PETERSON. (*crossing to WATERS*) C.J. couldn't hurt a fly, Waters, you know that!

WATERS. I found a gun, Soldier. (*He starts to cross*

s.l.; *PETERSON steps in front of him.*) — now get out of the way!

PETERSON. Goddamnit, Waters, you know it ain't him!

WATERS. How do I know?

HENSON. Right before you came in, I thought I saw somebody sneak in. (*He crosses* D.S. *towards WATERS.*)

WATERS. You were drunk when you left the Club (*WILKIE pushes HENSON* U.S. *He stumbles and sits on the* U.R.C. *bunk.*) — I saw you myself!

WILKIE. Besides, how you know it wasn't C.J.?

COBB. (*crossing* D.S. *toward Center*) I was here all night, C.J. didn't go out.

WATERS. (*looking at them, intensely*) We got the right man. (*points at C.J., impassioned*) You think he's innocent don't you? C.J. Memphis playin', cotton-picker, singin' the Blues, bowin' and scrapin' — smilin' in everybody's face — this man undermined us! You and me! The description of the man who did the shooting fits C.J.! (*to HENSON*) You saw C.J. sneak in here! (*points*) Don't be fooled — that yassah boss is hidin' something — Niggahs ain't like that today! This is 1943 — He shot that white boy! (*C.J. is stunned, then suddenly the enormity of his predicament hits him and he breaks free of WILKIE, and hits WATERS in the chest. The blow knocks him down, and C.J. is immediately grabbed by the other men in the barracks. COBB goes to WATERS and helps him up slowly. The blow hurt WATERS, but he forces a smile at C.J. who has suddenly gone immobile, surprised by what he has done.*) What did you go and do now, boy? Hit a non-commissioned officer.

COBB. Sarge, he didn't mean it! (*COBB picks up WATER'S cap.*)

WATERS. Shut up! (*He snatches his cap, and straightens up.*) Take him out, Wilkie.

(*C.J. crosses to* U.C. *bunk; opens lid and takes out his shirt, pants and boots. He exits calmly almost passively* S.L. *WILKIE follows him off. WATERS looks at all the men quietly for a moment, then walks out without saying a word. There is a momentary silence in the barracks.*)

SMALLS. Niggah like that can't have a mother.

HENSON. I know I saw something! (*He turns* U.S. *and looks at* U.C. *bunk, trying to recall what he saw. He then crosses and sits on the* R.C. *bunk.*)

PETERSON. C.J. was sleepin' when I came in! (*SMALLS crosses and sits on the* U.C. *Box. COBB crosses to* U.L. *Box and sits.*) It's Waters — can't y'all see that? (*He crosses to the* S.L. *Box; opens the lid and takes out pants, shirt, cap and boots. During the speech he dresses.*) I've seen him before — we had 'em in Alabama! White man gives them a little-ass job as a servant — close to the big house, and when the "boss" ain't lookin' old copy-cat nigahs act like they the new owner! They take to soundin' like the boss — shoutin', orderin' people aroun' — and when it comes to you and me — they sell us to continue favor. They think the "high-jailers" like that. Arrestin' C.J. — that'll get Waters another stripe! Next it'll be you — or you — he can't look good unless he's standin' on you! Cobb tol' him C.J. was in all evening — Waters didn' even listen! Turning somebody in (*He begins to put on boots. Mimics:*) "Look what I done, Captain-Boss!" They let him in the Army 'cause they know he'll do anything they tell him to — I've seen his kind of fool before. Someone's going to kill him.

SMALLS. (*standing*) I heard they killed a Sergeant at Fort Robinson—recruit did it—(*He crosses* U.R.; *sits on the* U.L.C. *Box.*)

COBB. It'll just be our luck, Sarge'll come through the whole war without a scratch.

PETERSON. Maybe—but I'm goin' over to the stockade—tell the MP's what I know. (*He puts on cap, crosses above* S.L. *Box.*) C.J. was here all evening!

SMALLS. I'll go with you!

COBB. Me too, I guess. (*They begin to dress as the light fades slowly in the barracks area. They exit* S.L. *as the lights come up full on DAVENPORT and HENSON.*)

DAVENPORT. (*crossing* C.) Could the person you thought you saw have stayed in the barracks—did you actually see someone go out?

HENSON. Yes, Sir!

DAVENPORT. Was Wilkie the only man out of his bunk that night?

HENSON. Guess so—he came in with Sarge.

DAVENPORT. And Peterson—he did most of the talking?

HENSON. As I recall. It's been awhile ago—an' I was juiced!

DAVENPORT. Ellis!

ELLIS. (*enters*) Sir!

DAVENPORT. I want Private Wilkie and PFC Peterson to report to me at once.

ELLIS. They're probably on work detail, Sir.

DAVENPORT. Find them.

ELLIS. Yes, Sir! (*ELLIS exits quickly and DAVENPORT, crossing* D.R., *lapses into a quiet thoughtfulness.*)

HENSON. Is there anything else?—Sir?

DAVENPORT. (*vexed*) No! That'll be all—send in the next man.

(*HENSON comes to "attention" and salutes. DAVEN-PORT returns it as HENSON exits* S.L. *crossing above* S.L. *bunk C.J.'s music plays in background. There is a silence, DAVENPORT crosses* D.L. *mumbling something inaudible to himself. COBB enters* S.L. *crosses below* S.L. *bunk to* S.L. *platform. He watches DAVENPORT for a moment.*)

COBB. Sir? (*DAVENPORT faces him.*) Corporal Cobb reporting as ordered, Sir. (*He salutes.*)

DAVENPORT. Have a seat, Corporal. (*COBB crosses* S.R. *and sits* S.R.C. *bunk. DAVENPORT crosses to* C.) And lets get something straight from the beginning—I don't care whether you like officers or not—is that clear? (*COBB looks at him strangely.*)

COBB. Sir? (*Pause. DAVENPORT calms somewhat.*)

DAVENPORT. I'm sorry—Did you know Sergeant Waters well?

COBB. As well as the next man, Sir—I was already with the team when he took over. Me and C.J., we made the team the same time.

DAVENPORT. Were you close to C.J.?

COBB. Me and him were "homeys", Sir! Both came from Mississippi. C.J. from Carmella—me, I'm from up 'roun Jutlerville, what they call "snake" County. Plus we both played for the Negro League before the war.

DAVENPORT. How did you feel about his arrest?

COBB. Terrible—C.J. didn't kill nobody, Sir.

DAVENPORT. He struck Sergeant Waters—

COBB. Waters made him, Sir! He called that boy things he had never heard of before—C.J., he was so confused he didn't know what else to do—(*pause*) An' when they put him in the stockade, he jus' seemed to go to pieces. (*DAVENPORT crosses* D.S.L. *below* S.L. *platform.*) See, we both lived on farms—and even though C.J.'s Daddy played music, C.J., he liked the wide open spaces. (*shakes his head*) That cell? It started closin' in on him right away. (*Blue-grey light rises in limbo area. C.J. enters* U.L. *carrying a chair. He sits* C. *of limbo area. A shadow of bars cuts across the space, as the lights* D.S. *dim.*) I went to see him, the second day he was in there. He looked pale and ashy, Sir—like something dead.

C.J. (*facing COBB*) It's hard to breathe in these little spaces, Cobb—man wasn' made for this hea'—nothin' was! I don't think I'll eva' see a' animal in a cage agin' and not feel sorry for it. (*to himself:*) I'd rather be on the chain-gang.

COBB. Come on, Homey! (*He rises, crosses to* L. *of limbo area.*)

C.J. I don't think I'm comin' outta' here, Cobb—feels like I'm goin' crazy. Can't walk in hea'—can't see the Sun! I tried singin', Cobb, but nothin' won't come out. I sure don't wanna' die in this jail!

COBB. (*moving closer*) Ain't nobody gonna' die, C.J.!

C.J. Yesterday I broke a guitar string—lost my Dust! I got no protection—nothin' to keep the dog from tearin' at my bones!

COBB. Stop talkin' crazy! (*C.J. is quiet for a moment. He stares forward.*)

C.J. You know, he come up hea' las' night? Sergeant Waters?

(*WATERS enters* U.L. *smoking a pipe. He crosses up ramp to limbo area and stands* L. *of C.J.*)

WATERS. (*calmly*) You should learn never to hit Sergeants, boy—man can get in a lot of trouble doin' that kinda' thing durin' war time—they talkin' 'bout givin' you five years—they call what you did mutiny in the Navy. Mutiny, boy.

C.J. That gun ain't mine!

WATERS. Oh, we know that, C.J.! (*C.J. is surprised. WATERS crosses L. sits U.L.C. bunk.*) That gun belonged to the Niggah did the shootin' over at Williams place—me and Wilkie caught him hidin' in the Motor Pool, and he confessed his head off. You're in here for striking a superior officer, boy. And I got a whole barracks full of your friends to prove it! (*smiles broadly, as C.J. shakes his head*)

DAVENPORT. (*to COBB at once*) Memphis wasn't charged with the shooting?

COBB. No, Sir—

WATERS. Don't feel too bad, boy. It's not your fault entirely—it has to be this way. The First War, it didn't change much for us, boy—but this one—it's gonna' change a lot of things. Them Nazis ain't all crazy—a whole lot of people just can't fit into where things seem to be goin'—like you, C.J. The black race can't afford you no more. There useta' be a time when we'd see somebody like you, singin', clownin',—yas-sah-bossin' —and we wouldn't do anything. (*smiles*) Folks liked that—you were a good—homey kinda' Niggah—they needed somebody to mistreat—call a name, they paraded you, reminded them of the old days—cornbread bakin', greens and ham cookin'—Daddy out pickin' cotton, Grandmammy sittin' on the front porch smokin' a pipe. (*slight pause*) Not no more. The day of the geechy is gone, boy—the only thing that can move the race is power. It's all the white respects—and people like you just make us seem like fools. And we can't let nobody go

on believin', we all like you! You bring us down — make
people think the whole race is unfit! (*He rises.*) I waited
a long time for you, boy, but I gotcha'! And I try to git
rid of you wherever I go. I put two "geechies" in jail at
Fort Campbell, Kentucky — three at Fort Huachuca.
Now I got you — one less fool for the race to be ashamed
of! (*rises, crosses to C.J.*) And I'ma git that ole' boy
Cobb next! (*WATERS exits* us.l. *ramp.*)

DAVENPORT. (*at once*) You?

COBB. Yes, Sir. (*slight pause*)

DAVENPORT. Go on.

C.J. You imagin' anybody sayin' that? I know I'm not
gittin' outta' hea', Cobb! (*quiets*) You remember I tol'
you 'bout a place I useta' go outside Carmella? When I
was a little ole' tiny thing? Place out behind O'Connell's
Farm? Place would be stinkin' of plums, Cobb.
Shaded — that ripe smell be weavin' through the cotton
fields and clear on inta' town on a warm day. First time
I had Evelyn? I had her unda' them plum trees. I wrote
a song for her — (*talks, sings*) My ginger colored
Moma — she had thighs the size of hams! (*chuckles*)
And when you spread them Momaaaa!/(*talks*) You let
me have my jelly roll and jam! (*pause, mood swing*)
O'Connell, he had a dog — meanes' dog I *eva'* did see!
An' the only way you could enjoy them plum trees was
to outsmart that dog. Waters is like that ole' dog,
Cobb — you gotta' run circles roun' ole Windy — that was
his name. They say he tore a man's arm off once, and
got to likin' it. So, you had to cheat that dog outta' bitin'
you every time. Every time. (*Slowly the light begins to
fade around C.J. as he exits* u.s.l. *ramp with chair.*)

COBB. He didn't make sense, Sir (*He crosses to* u.r.c.
bunk; sits.) I tried talkin' about the team — the

War — ain't nothin' work — seem like he jes' got worse.

DAVENPORT. What happened to him? (*COBB looks at him, incredulously.*)

COBB. The next day — afta' the day I saw him? C.J. he hung hisself, Sir! Suicide — jes' couldn't stand it. MP's found him hung from the bars. (*DAVENPORT is silent for a moment then crosses* U.L.C.)

DAVENPORT. What happened after that?

COBB. We lost our last game — we jes' "threw" it — we did it for C.J. — Captain he was mad 'cause we ain't git ta' play the Yankees. Peterson was right on that one — somebody needed to protest that man!

DAVENPORT. What did Waters do?

COBB. Well afta' we lost, the Commanding Officer, he broke up the team, and we all got re-assigned to this Smoke Company. Waters, he started actin' funny, Sir — stayed drunk — talked to hisself all the time.

DAVENPORT. Did you think you were next?

COBB. I ain't sure I eva' believed Waters said that, Sir — C.J. had to be outta' his head or he wouldna' killed hisself — Sarge, he neva' came near me afta' C.J. died.

DAVENPORT. What time did you get back the night Waters was killed?

COBB. I'd say between 2120 and 9:30. (*DAVENPORT crosses* D.R.)

DAVENPORT. And you didn't go out again?

COBB. No, Sir — me and Henson sat and listened to the radio 'til Abbott and Lou Costella went off, then I played checkers with Wilkie for 'notha' hour, then everybody went to bed. — What C.J. said about Waters? It ain't botha' me, Sir. (*DAVENPORT is silent.*)

DAVENPORT. Who were the last ones in that night?

COBB. Smalls and Peterson — they had Guard Duty.

(*TAYLOR enters the barracks area and stops just inside the door* s.l.*, when he sees DAVENPORT isn't quite finished. He carries a clipboard with papers attached.*)

DAVENPORT. Thank you, Corporal. (*COBB rises at "attention" and salutes. DAVENPORT returns it and COBB crosses* s.l. *He salutes TAYLOR, who returns it. COBB exits* s.l. *TAYLOR advances toward DAVENPORT.*)

TAYLOR. (*smiling*) You surprise me, Davenport — I just left Colonel Nivens. He's given you permission to question Byrd and Wilcox? (*DAVENPORT nods.*) How'd you manage that? (*TAYLOR crosses* D.L.C.) You threatened him with an article in the Chicago Defender, I suppose.

DAVENPORT. I convinced the Colonel it was in his best interests to allow it.

TAYLOR. Really? Did he tell you I would assist you?

DAVENPORT. I told him I especially didn't want you. (*DAVENPORT crosses* C. *to TAYLOR.*)

TAYLOR. That's precisely why he sent me — he didn't want you to think you could get your way entirely — not with him. Then neither Byrd or Wilcox would submit to it without a white officer present. That's how it is. (*There is a rather long silence.*) But there's something else, Davenport. The Colonel began talking about the affidavits he and the others signed — and the discrepancies in their statements that night. (*mimics*) He wants me with you because he doesn't want Byrd and Wilcox giving you the "wrong impression" — he never elaborated on what he meant by the "wrong impression." I want to be there!

DAVENPORT. So you're not on *that* side anymore—you're on *my* side now, right? (*DAVENPORT crosses* s.l. *below TAYLOR who counters.*)

TAYLOR. (*bristles*) I want whoever killed my Sergeant, Davenport!

DAVENPORT. Bullshit! Yesterday you were daring me to try! And today we're allies? Besides you don't give that much of a damn about your men! I've been around you a full day and you haven't uttered a word that would tell me you had any more than a minor acquaintance with Waters! He managed your baseball team—was an NCO in your company, and you haven't offered *any* opinion of the man as a soldier —Sergeant—platoon leader! Who the hell was he?

TAYLOR. He was one of my men! On my roster—a man these bars make me responsible for! And no, I don't know a helluva' lot about him—or a lot of their names or where they come from, but I'm still their Commanding Officer and in a little while I may have to trust them with my life! And I want them to know they can trust me with theirs—here and now! (*pause*) I have Byrd and Wilcox in my office. (*DAVENPORT stares at him for a long moment. TAYLOR crosses* D.S.L. *DAVENPORT counters. BYRD and WILCOX enter* D.R. *cross up ramp to* S.R. *platform. BYRD and WILCOX sit in chairs* S.L. *and* S.R. *of table, respectively. BOTH are in dress uniform.*) Why didn't you tell Nivens that you'd placed me under arrest? (*DAVENPORT stops.*)

DAVENPORT. I didn't find it necessary. (*They stare at one another. TAYLOR is noticeably strained. DAVENPORT crosses* D.L.C. *looking at notes.*) What do you know about C.J. Memphis? (*TAYLOR crosses to* C. *toward DAVENPORT.*)

TAYLOR. (*shrugs*) He was a big man as I recall—more

a boy than a man, though. Played the guitar sometimes at the Officer's Club—there was something embarrassing about him. Committed suicide in the stockade. Pretty good centerfielder—(*DAVENPORT stops.*)

DAVENPORT. Did you investigate his arrest—the charges against him?

TAYLOR. He was charged with assaulting a non-commissioned officer—I questioned him—he didn't say much. He admitted he struck Waters—I started questioning several of the men in the platoon and he killed himself before I could finish—open and shut case.

DAVENPORT. I think Waters tricked C.J. into assaulting him.

TAYLOR. Waters wasn't that kind of a man! He admitted he might have provoked the boy—he accused him of that Golden Palace shooting—Listen, Waters didn't have a fifth grade education—he wasn't a schemer! And colored soldiers aren't devious like that.

DAVENPORT. What do you mean we aren't devious?

TAYLOR. (*sharply*) You're not as devious—! (*DAVENPORT stares as TAYLOR waves disdainfully and starts into the office, crossing onto* S.L. *platform. He then crosses* S.R. *on this level to* S.L. *platform. DAVENPORT follows.*)—Anyway, what has that to do with this? (*He is distracted by BYRD and WILCOX before DAVENPORT can answer. TAYLOR speaks as he places his clipboard on* U.R.C. *Box.*) This is *Captain* Davenport—you've both been briefed by Colonel Nivens to give the Captain your full cooperation. (*DAVENPORT crosses to* D.L. *of WILCOX, stands facing them.*)

BYRD. (*To DAVENPORT*) They tell me you a lawyer, huh?

DAVENPORT. I am not here to answer your questions,

Lieutenant. And I am Captain Davenport, is that clear?

BYRD. (*to TAYLOR*) Captain, is he crazy?

TAYLOR. You got your orders.

BYRD. Sir, I vigorously protest as an Officer—

TAYLOR. (*cutting him off*) You answer him the way he wants you to, Byrd, or I'll have your ass in a sling so tight, you won't be able to pee, soldier! (*BYRD backs off slightly.*)

DAVENPORT. When did you last see Sergeant Waters?

BYRD. The night he was killed, but I didn' kill him—I should have blown his head off, the way he spoke to me and Captain Wilcox here.

DAVENPORT. How did he speak to you, Captain?

WILCOX. Well, he was very drunk—and he said a lot of things he shouldn't have. I told the Lieutenant here not to make the situation worse and he agreed, and we left the Sergeant on his knees wallowing in self-pity. (*shrugs*)

DAVENPORT. What exactly did he say?

WILCOX. Some pretty stupid things about us—I mean white people, Sir. (*BYRD reacts to the term "Sir".*)

DAVENPORT. What kind of things?

BYRD. (*annoyed*) He said he wasn't going to obey no white man's orders! And that me and Wilcox here were to blame for him being black, and not able to sleep or keep his food down! And I didn't even know the man! Never even spoke to him before that night!

DAVENPORT. Anything else?

WILCOX. Well—he said he'd killed somebody.

DAVENPORT. Did he call a name—or say who?

WILCOX. Not that I recall, Sir. (*DAVENPORT looks at BYRD.*)

BYRD. No—(*sudden and sharp*) Look—the goddamn Negro was disrespectful! He wouldn't salute! Wouldn't come to attention! And where I come from colored don't talk the way he spoke to us—not to white people they don't!

DAVENPORT. Is that the reason you killed him?

BYRD. I killed nobody! I said, "where I come from!" didn't I? You'd be dead yourself, where I come from! But I didn't kill the—the *Negro!*

DAVENPORT. But you hit him, didn't you?

BYRD. I knocked him down!

DAVENPORT. (*quickens pace*) And when you went to look at him he was dead, wasn't he?

BYRD. He was alive when we left!

DAVENPORT. You're a liar! You beat Waters up—you went back and you shot him!

BYRD. No! (*rising*) But you better get outta' my face before I kill *you!* (*DAVENPORT stands firm.*)

DAVENPORT. Like you killed Waters?

BYRD. No! (*He rises, crosses threateningly to DAV-ENPORT.*)

TAYLOR. (*at once*) Soldier!

BYRD. He's trying to put it on me!

TAYLOR. Answer his questions, Lieutenant. (*BYRD sits.*)

DAVENPORT. You were both coming off bivouac, right?

WILCOX. Yes.

DAVENPORT. So you both had weapons?

BYRD. So what? We didn't fire them!

DAVENPORT. Were the weapons turned in immediately?

WILCOX. Yes, Sir—Colonel Nivens took our .45's to Major Hines. It was all kept quiet because the Colonel didn't want the colored boys to know that anyone white from the Fort was involved in any way — ballistics cleared them.

DAVENPORT. We can check.

BYRD. Go ahead.

TAYLOR. I don't believe it — why wasn't I told?

WILCOX. The weapons had cleared — and the Colonel felt if he involved you further, you'd take the matter to Washington and there'd be a scandel about colored and white soldiers — as it turned out, he thinks you went to Washington anyway. (*He rises, faces DAVENPORT.*) I'd like to say, Captain, that neither Lieutenant Byrd or myself had anything whatsoever to do with Sergeant Waters' death — I swear that as an officer and a gentleman. He was on the ground when we left him, but very much alive.

TAYLOR. Consider yourselves under arrest, *Gentlemen!*

BYRD. Oh what charge?

TAYLOR. Murder! You think I believe that crap —

DAVENPORT. Let them go, Captain.

TAYLOR. You've got a motive — a witness to their being at the scene —

DAVENPORT. Let them go! This is still my investigation — you two are dismissed! (*BYRD rises quickly, WILCOX follows his lead.*)

WILCOX. Are we being charged, Sir?

DAVENPORT. Not by me.

WILCOX. Thank you. (*WILCOX comes to attention, joined by a reluctant BYRD. They both salute. DAVENPORT returns it. They start out.*)

BYRD. I expected more from a white man, Captain.

TAYLOR. Get out of here, before I have you cashiered out of the Army, Byrd! (*Both men exit quietly down* s.r. *ramp. For a moment, TAYLOR and DAVEN-PORT are quiet. Then TAYLOR crosses to desk sits L. chair.*) What the hell is the matter with you? You could have charged both of them—Byrd for insubordination —Wilcox—tampering with evidence.

DAVENPORT. Neither charge is murder—you think Wilcox would tell a story like that if he didn't have Hines and Nivens to back it up? (*slightly tired*) They've got a report.

TAYLOR. So what do you do now?

DAVENPORT. Finish the investigation.

TAYLOR. They're lying, damnit! So is the Colonel! You were ordered to investigate and charge the people responsible—charge them! I'll back you up!

DAVENPORT. I'm not satisfied yet, Captain.

TAYLOR. I am! Damnit! (*He rises, and crosses s.l. in office area.*)—I wish they'd sent somebody else! I do—You—you're afraid! You thought you'd accuse the Klan, didn't you?—and that would be the end of it, right? Another story of midnight riders for your Negro Press! And now it's officers—white men in the Army. It's too much for you—what will happen when Captain Davenport comes up for promotion to Major if he accuses white officers, right?

DAVENPORT. I'm not afraid of white men, Captain.

TAYLOR. Then why the hell won't you arrest them?

DAVENPORT. Because I do what the facts tell me, Captain—not you!

TAYLOR. You don't know what a fact is, Davenport!

(*ELLIS enters suddenly s.r. crosses up ramp to u.l. of s.l. chairs.*)

ELLIS. Begging your pardon, Sir.

TAYLOR. What is it, Corporal?

ELLIS. Ah—it's for Captain Davenport—(*ELLIS crosses* DS.R. *to DAVENPORT; TAYLOR crosses* S.L.) We found Private Wilkie, Sir. We haven't located Pfc. Peterson yet. Seems him and Private Smalls went out on "detail" together, and neither one of 'em showed up—but I got a few men from the Company lookin' for 'em around the NCO Club and in the PX, sir.

DAVENPORT. Where's Wilkie?

ELLIS. He's waiting for you in the barracks, Captain. (*DAVENPORT nods, and ELLIS goes out after saluting. DAVENPORT returns the salute then crosses to the table and reviews the notes in his folder.*)

TAYLOR. Didn't you question Wilkie and Peterson yesterday? Davenport? (*DAVENPORT does not answer. TAYLOR crosses to the table and slams his hand on DAVENPORT'S notes.*) Don't you ignore me!

DAVENPORT. Get off my back! What I do—how I do it—who I interrogate is my business, Captain! This investigation is mine! (*pause*) Mine!

TAYLOR. Don't treat me with that kind of contempt—I'm not some red-neck cracker!

DAVENPORT. And I'm not your yessirin' colored boy either!

TAYLOR. I asked you a question!

DAVENPORT. I don't have to answer it! (*There is a long silence, the two men glare at one another.*)

TAYLOR. (*disturbed*) Indeed you don't—*Captain*. (*Pause. He sits in* S.L. *chair.*)

DAVENPORT. Now, *Captain*—what if Byrd and Wilcox are telling the truth?

TAYLOR. Neither one of us believes that.

DAVENPORT. What if they are? (*He sits* S.R. *chair.*)
TAYLOR. Then who killed the goddamn man?

(*WILKIE enters* S.L. *with Negro newspaper as the lights begin to rise in the barracks area. WILKIE crosses to* L.C. *bunk, sits and begins to read.*)

DAVENPORT. I don't know yet. (*slight pause*) Is there anything else?
TAYLOR. No, hot shot. Nothing. (*He rises, picks up his clipboard, and exits* S.R. *down ramp.*)

(*DAVENPORT crosses* S.L. *into barracks area. WILKIE quickly puts his paper aside and snaps-to "attention" and salutes. DAVENPORT returns it. The light around the office fades out.*)

DAVENPORT. (*snapping at WILKIE*) When did you lose your stripes?
WILCOX. Couple months before they broke up the team—right after Sergeant Waters got assigned to us, Sir.
DAVENPORT. Nervous, Wilkie?
WILKIE. (*smiling haltingly*) I couldn't figure out why you called me back, Sir? (*He laughs nervously.*)
DAVENPORT. (*crossing* S.L.) You lost your stripes for being drunk on duty, is that correct?
WILKIE. Yes, Sir. (*He sits* U.L.C. *bunk.*)
DAVENPORT. You said Waters busted you, didn't you?
WILKIE. He got me busted—he's the one reported me to the Captain.
DAVENPORT. How did you feel? Must have been awful—(*He paces.*) Weren't you and the Sergeant good friends? Didn't you tell me he was alright? A nice guy?

WILKIE. Yes, Sir.

DAVENPORT. Would a nice guy have gotten a friend busted?

WILKIE. No, Sir.

DAVENPORT. So you lied when you said he was a nice guy, right? (*He crosses* S.L.)

WILKIE. No, Sir—I mean—

DAVENPORT. Speak up! Speak up! Was the Sergeant a nice guy or not?

WILKIE. No, Sir.

DAVENPORT. Why not? Answer me!

WILKIE. Well, you wouldn't turn somebody in over something like that!

DAVENPORT. Not a good friend, right?

WILKIE. Right, Sir—I mean a friend would give you extra duty—I would have—or even call you a whole buncha' names—you'd expect that, Sir—but damn! Three stripes? They took ten years to get in this Army, Sir! Ten years! I started out with the 24th Infantry—I—

DAVENPORT. Made you mad didn't it?

WILKIE. Yeah, it made me mad—all the things I did for him!

DAVENPORT. (*quickly*) That's right! You were his assistant, weren't you? Took care of the team—(*WILKIE nods.*) Ran all his errands, looked at his family snapshots, (*WILKIE nods again.*) policed his quarters, put the gun under C.J.'s bed—(*WILKIE looks up suddenly.*)

WILKIE. No!

DAVENPORT. (*quickly*) It was you Henson saw, wasn't it, Wilkie?

WILKIE. No, Sir!

DAVENPORT. Liar! You lied about Waters, and you're lying now! You were the only person out of the barracks that night, and the only one who knew the layout well enough to go straight to C.J.'s bunk! Not even Waters knew the place that well! Henson didn't see who it was, but he saw what the person did—he was positive about that—only you knew the barracks in the dark! (*He crosses* s.r.)

WILKIE. (*pleadingly*) It was the Sarge, Captain—he ordered me to do it—he said I'd get my stripes back—he wanted to scare that boy C.J.! Let him stew in jail! Then C.J. hit him—and he had the boy right where he wanted him—(*confused*) But it backfired—C.J. killed hisself—Sarge didn't figure on that.

DAVENPORT. (*crossing* s.l. *to WILKIE*) Why did he pick Memphis?

WILKIE. He despised him, Captain—he'd hide it, 'cause everybody in the company liked that boy so much. But underneath—It was a crazy hate, Sir—he'd go cold when he talked about C.J. You could feel it.

(*DAVENPORT crosses* ds.r. *on Level A, as WATERS and C.J. enter* u.s.l. *and* u.s.r. *ramps, respectively. C.J. plays a soft blues tune on his guitar as he stands* u.r. *in limbo area. WATERS crosses* d.l. *in the limbo area, smoking his pipe and talks to WILKIE, as the blue-grey light rises on him and C.J. and the lights in the barracks area dims. Specials highlight DAVENPORT and WILKIE.*)

WATERS. He's the kinda' boy seems innocent, Wilkie. Got everybody around the Post thinking he's a strong, black buck! Hits homeruns—white boys envy his strength—his speed, the power in his swing. Then this colored champion lets those same white boys call him "Shine"—or "Sambo" at the Officers' Club. They laugh at his blues songs, and he just smiles—can't talk, barely

read or write his own name—and don't care! He'll tell
you they like him—or that colored folks ain't supposed
to have but so much sense. (*intense*) Do you know the
damage one ignorant *Negro* can do? (*Remembering,
WATERS crosses* D.L.C. *in limbo area.*) We were in
France during the First War, Wilkie. We had won
decorations, but the white boys had told all the French
gals we had tails. And they found this ignorant colored
soldier. Paid him to tie a tail to his ass and parade
around naked making monkey sounds. (*shakes his
head.*) They sat him on a big, round table in the Café
Napoleon, put a reed in his hand, a crown on his head, a
blanket on his shoulders and made him eat bananas in
front of them Frenchies. And ohhh, the white boys
danced that night—passed out leaflets with that boy's
picture on them—called him "Moonshine, King of the
Monkeys." And when we slit his throat, you know that
fool asked us, what he had done wrong? (*pause*) My
Daddy told me, we got to turn our backs on his kind,
Wilkie. Close our ranks to the chittlin's, the collard
greens—the cornbread style. We are men—soldiers, and
I don't intend to have our race cheated out of its place of
honor and respect in *this* War because of fools like C.J.!
You watch everything he does—*Everything!*

(*C.J. and WATERS exit* US.R. *and* US.L. *ramp, respectively, as the light in the limbo area fades.
C.J. stops playing, as the light rises in the barracks
area.*)

WILKIE. And I watched him, Sir—but Waters—he
couldn't wait! He wouldn't talk about nothin' else—it
was C.J., this—C.J. all the time!
DAVENPORT. (*troubled, DAVENPORT crosses*

toward WILKIE.) Why didn't he pick Peterson—they fought—

WILKIE. They fought all the time, Sir—but the Sarge, he liked Peterson. (*nods*) Peterson fought back, and Waters admired that. He promoted Pete! Imagine that—he thought Peterson would make a "fine" soldier!

DAVENPORT. What was Peterson's reaction—when C.J. died?

WILKIE. Like everybody else, he was sad—he put together that protest that broke up the team but afta' that he didn' say much. And he usually runs off at the mouth. Kept to himself—or with Smalls. (*Slight pause. DAVENPORT crosses D.L. on S.L. platform.*)

DAVENPORT. The night Waters was killed, what time did you get in?

WILKIE. Around 9:45—couple of us came from the Club and listened to the radio awhile—I played some checkers, then I went to bed. Sir? I didn't mean to do what I did—it wasn't my fault—he promised me my stripes!

(*Suddenly out of nowhere in the near distance is the sound of gunfire, a bugle blaring, something like a cannon going off. The noise is continuous through scene. DAVENPORT crosses S.R.*)

DAVENPORT. I'm placing you under arrest, Private!

(*ELLIS bursts into the room from S.L. and crosses to DAVENPORT.*)

ELLIS. Did you hear, Sir? (*DAVENPORT, surprised, shakes his "no".*) Our orders! They came down from Washington, Captain! We're shippin' out! They finally gonna' let us Negroes fight! (*DAVENPORT is immediately elated, and almost forgets WILKIE   as he shakes ELLIS' hand. WILKIE rises.*)

DAVENPORT. Axis ain't got a chance!

ELLIS. Surrrre—we'll win this mother in six months now! Afta' what Jesse Owens did to them people? Joe Louis?

(*HENSON bursts in from s.l. and crosses to ELLIS.*)

HENSON. Did y'all hear it? 48 hour stand-by alert! We goin' into combat! (*HENSON takes cap off and crosses* D.C. *elatedly. Loudly:*) Look out, Hitler, the niggahs is comin' to git your ass through the fog!

ELLIS. With real rifles—it's really OK, you know?

HENSON. They tell me them girls in England— woooow! (*HENSON twirls his cap on his finger. DAVENPORT faces WILKIE as COBB enters from s.l. yelling and crosses to* D.L.C.)

COBB. They gonna' let us git in it! We may lay so much smoke the Germans may never get to see what a colored soldier looks like 'til the War's over! (*to HENSON:*) I wrote my woman jes' the otha' day that we'd be goin' soon!

ELLIS. Go on!

HENSON. (*overlapping*) Man, you ain't write nothin'! (*WILKIE crosses* s.r. *to DAVENPORT.*) If the Army said we was all discharged, you'd claim you wrote that! (*He quiets watching DAVENPORT.*)

COBB. (*quickly*) You hea' this fool, Sir?

HENSON. Shhhhh!

DAVENPORT. (*to ELLIS*) Corporal, escort Private Wilkie to the stockade.

ELLIS. (*surprised*) Yes, Sir! (*ELLIS starts WILKIE*

out, even though he is bewildered by it. They exit S.L.
HENSON crosses to DAVENPORT.)

HENSON. Wilkie's under arrest, Sir? (*DAVENPORT
nods.*) How come? I apologize, Sir — I didn't mean that.

DAVENPORT. Do either of you know where Smalls and
Peterson can be located? (*HENSON shrugs.*)

COBB. Your men got Smalls in the stockade, Sir!

DAVENPORT. When?

COBB. I saw two colored MP's takin' him through the
main gate. Jes' awhile ago — I was on my way ova' hea'!
(*DAVENPORT starts out* S.L. *crossing below* S.L.
bunk.) Tenn-hut! (*DAVENPORT stops and salutes.*)

DAVENPORT. As you were — by the way — congratula-
tions! (*DAVENPORT exits the barracks* S.L.)

HENSON. Look out, Hitler!

COBB. The Niggahs is coming, to get yo' ass.

HENSON & COBB. Through the fog.

(*HENSON and COBB exit* S.L. *shooting imaginary
machine guns as the lights in the barracks go down.
Simultaneously, they rise in limbo as SMALLS
enters* US.L. *up the ramp, smoking a cigarette. The
shadow of bars fall over his cell. In the background
the sounds of celebration continue. DAVENPORT
enters* D.R. *crosses up the* S.R. *ramp and stands* S.R.
*of limbo area. He begins immediately as the noises
of celebration fade in the background.*)

DAVENPORT. Why'd you go AWOL, soldier?
(*SMALL faces him, unable to see DAVENPORT at
first. When he sees him, he extinguishes his cigarette,
snaps to attention and salutes.*)

SMALLS. Private Anthony Smalls, Sir!

DAVENPORT. At ease — answer my question!

SMALLS. I didn't go AWOL, Sir — I — I got drunk in Tynin and fell asleep in the bus depot — it was the only public place I could find to sleep it off.

DAVENPORT. Where'd you get drunk? Where in Tynin?

SMALLS. Jakes — Jakes and Lilly's Golden Slipper — On Melville Street —

DAVENPORT. Weren't you and Peterson supposed to be on detail? (*SMALLS nods.*) Where was Peterson? Speak up!

SMALLS. I don't know, Sir!

DAVENPORT. You're lying! You just walked off your detail and Peterson did nothing?

SMALLS. No, Sir — he warned me, Sir — "Listen, Smalls!" He said —

DAVENPORT. (*cutting him off*) You trying to make a fool of me, Smalls? Huh? (*loudly*) Are you?

SMALLS. No, Sir!

DAVENPORT. The two of you went A-W-O-L together, didn't you? (*SMALLS is quiet.*) Answer me!

SMALLS. Yes!

DAVENPORT. You left together because Peterson knew I would find out the two of you killed Waters, didn' you? (*SMALLS begins to pace nervously.*) What? I can't hear you! (*SMALLS is sobbing.*) You killed Waters didn't you? I want an answer!

SMALLS. I can't sleep — I can't sleep!

DAVENPORT. Did you kill Sergeant Waters?

SMALLS. It was Peterson, Sir! (*as if he can see it*) I watched! It wasn't me!

(*The blue-grey light builds in C.S. As it does, SER-
    GEANT WATERS staggers into limbo area from
    U.S.R. ramp and falls on his knees. He can't get up*

he is so drunk, he has been beaten, and looks the way we saw him in the opening of the First Act.)

SMALLS. (*continued*) We were changing the guard.

WATERS. Can't be trusted—no matter what we do, there are no guarantees— and your mind won't let you forget it. (*shakes his head repeatedly*) No, no, no!

SMALLS. (*overlapping*) On our way back to the Captain's office—and Sarge, he was on the road. We just walked into him! He was ranting, and acting crazy, Sir!

(*PETERSON enters* US.L. *ramp into the limbo area. He is dressed in a long coat, pistol belt and pistol, his pants bloused over his boots. He see WATERS and smiles. WATERS continues to babble.*)

PETERSON. Smalls, look who's drunk on his ass, boy! (*He begins to circle WATERS.*)

SMALLS. (*to DAVENPORT*) I told him to forget Waters! (*He crosses* U.C.)

PETERSON. Noooo! (*He crosses* S.R.) I'm gonna' enjoy this, Smalls—big, bad Sergeant Waters down on his knees? No, sah—I'm gonna' love this! (*He leans over WATERS.*) Hey, Sarge—need some help? (*WATERS looks up; almost smiles. He reaches for PETERSON who pushes him back down. Crossing* S.L.) That's the kinda' help I'll give yah, boy! Let me help you again —alright? (*PETERSON lifts WATERS and punches him several times. WATERS unsuccessfully tries to defend himself.*) Like that, Sarge? Huh? Like that, dog?

SMALLS. (*shouting*) Peterson!

PETERSON. No! (*almost pleading*) Smalls—some people, man—If this was a German would you kill it? If it was Hitler—or that fuckin' Tojo? Would you kill him? (*He kicks WATERS again.*)

WATERS. (*mumbling throughout*) There's a trick to it, Peterson—it's the only way you can win—C.J. could never make it—he was a clown! (*He grabs at PETERSON.*) A clown in blackface! A niggah! (*PETERSON steps out of reach. He is suddenly expressionless as he easily removes his pistol from his holster.*) You got to be like them! And I was! I was—but the rules are fixed. (*whispers*) Shhh! Listen. It's C.J.—C.J. and his music—(*laughs*) I made him do it, but it dosen't make any difference! They still hate you! (*Looks at PETERSON who has moved closer to him.*) They still hate you! (*WATERS laughs.*)

PETERSON. (*to SMALLS*) Justice, Smalls. (*He raises the pistol.*)

DAVENPORT. (*suddenly, harshly*) That isn't Justice! (*SMALLS almost recoils.*)

PETERSON. (*simultaneously, continuing*) For C.J.! Everybody!

WATERS. They still hate you!

(*PETERSON crosses away from WATERS and exits U.S.L. He fires the gun at WATERS' chest; and the shot stops everything. Even DAVENPORT in his way seems to hear it. PETERSON fires again. There is a moment of quiet onstage. DAVENPORT is angered and troubled.*)

DAVENPORT. You call that Justice?

SMALLS. No, Sir.

DAVENPORT. (*enraged*) Then why the fuck didn't you do something?

SMALLS. I'm scared of Peterson—Just scared of him! (*PETERSON enters U.S.L. putting pistol in his holster and crosses to WATERS. He begins to drag WATERS as best he can, and pull him offstage down the U.S.L.*)

ramp. It is done with some difficulty.) I tried to get him to go, Sir, but he wanted to drag the Sergeant's body back into the woods—

(*Light fades quickly around PETERSON, as DAVEN-PORT paces.*)

SMALLS. (*continued*) Said everybody would think white people did it.
DAVENPORT. (*somewhat drained*) Then what happened?
SMALLS. I got sick, Sir—and Peterson when he got done, he helped me back to the barracks and told me to keep quiet. (*slight pause*) I'm sorry, Sir. (*There is a long pause, during which DAVENPORT stares at SMALLS with disgust, then abruptly starts out without saluting. He almost flees.*) Sir?

(*DAVENPORT turns around. SMALLS comes to "attention" and salutes. DAVENPORT does not return it. He starts out of the cell and down the S.R. ramp. The lights fade around SMALLS. DAVENPORT, in deep thought crosses to C.S. as a special rises on him. DAVENPORT addresses the audience.*)

DAVENPORT. Peterson was apprehended a week later in Alabama. Colonel Nivens called it, "Just another black mess of cuttin', slashin' and shootin'!" He was delighted there were no white officers mixed-up in it, and his report to Washington characterized the events surrounding Waters' murder as, " . . . the usual, common violence any Commander faces in Negro Military Units." It was the kind of "mess" that turns up on page three in the colored papers—the Cain and Abel story of the week—the headline we Negroes can't quite read in comfort. (*shakes head and paces*) For me? Two colored soldiers are dead—two on their way to prison. (*pause*) The case got little attention. The details were filed in my report and I was quickly and rather unceremoniously ordered back to my MP unit. (*smiles*) A style of guitar-pickin' and a dance called the "C.J." caught on for awhile in Tynin saloons during 1945. (*slight pause*) In Northern New Jersey, through a military foul-up, Sergeant Waters' family was informed that he had been killed in action. The Sergeant was, therefore, thought and unofficially rumored to have been, the first colored casualty of the war from the county and under the circumstances was declared a hero. Nothing could be done officially, but his picture was hung on a "Wall-of Honor" in the Doris Miller VFW Post #978. (*pause*) The men of the 221st Chemical Smoke Generating Company? The entire outfit, officers and enlisted men were wiped out in the Ruhr Valley during a German advance. (*He turns toward TAYLOR who enters quietly* s.l. *as the lights come up full around them.*) Captain?

TAYLOR. Davenport—I see you got your man.

DAVENPORT. I got him—what is it, Captain?

TAYLOR. Will you accept my saying you did a splendid job?

DAVENPORT. I'll take the praise—but how did I manage it?

TAYLOR. Damnit, Davenport—I didn't come here to be made fun of—(*slight pause*) The men—the regiment —we all ship out for Europe tomorrow, and . . . (*He hesitates.*)

DAVENPORT. (*needling TAYLOR slyly*) You came to say good bye Captain?

TAYLOR. I was wrong, Davenport—about the bars—the uniform—about Negroes being in charge. (*slight pause*) I guess I'll *have* to get used to it.

DAVENPORT. (*smiling*) Oh, you'll get used to it—you can bet your ass on that. Captain—you will get used to it.

(*Lights begin to fade slowly as the 1940's popular song music from the start of the play begins to rise in the background, and the stage goes to black.*)

THE END.

March 4, 1941	WILKIE promoted to Staff Sgt. (C.J./COBB/WILKIE on baseball team)
1942	PETERSON enlisted in Army
March 5, 1943	WATERS assigned to 221st Company B. Placed in charge of team
May 1943	HENSON arrives in Co., placed on team
June 1943	PETERSON transferred to 221st Co. B., placed on team
June 1943	PETERSON and WATERS fight.
July 1943	WILKIE busted
Aug.–Sept. 1943	PETERSON promoted to Pfc.
September 1943	C.J. framed. (Shooting at Golden Palace.) C.J. in stockade. End of baseball season
3rd Day	C.J. commits suicide.
Sept. 1943	PETERSON organized protest. Team breaks up and reassigned.
April 1944	WATERS shot.

BYRD and WILCOX
   on bivouac
SMALLS and PETERSON
   on guard duty
TAYLOR Capt. of the
   Guard
COBB sees Waters fighting
   outside NCO Club — 9:00
BYRD and WILCOX
   leave Waters alive — 9:10
COBB and HENSON
   listen to radio in
   barracks — 9:20
BYRD and WILCOX
   in barracks — 9:30
WILKIE in barracks — 9:45

May 1944   DAVENPORT begins
   investigation
WILKIE arrested
SMALLS in stockade
PETERSON apprehended
   in Alabama
221st Chemical Smoke
   Generating Co. wiped
   out in Ruhr Valley

COSTUME LIST

SERGEANT WATERS
Full dress uniform (2, one soiled)
black shoes, black socks
Green fatigue pants
Green fatigue shirt
Khaki "cunt" cap
Black combat boots
helmet
MEDALS
Army Good Conduct
Soldier's Medal
Bronze Star
U.S. Cross Rifle

CAPTAIN TAYLOR
Full dress uniform
Hat
Black shoes
Black socks
Green fatigue pants
Green fatigue shirt
Khaki "cunt" cap
Black combat boots
MEDALS
Army Good Conduct
Dist. Service Medal-Army
Two Bars, U.S. Cross Rifle

CORPORAL COBBS
Green fatigue pants
Green fatigue shirt
Black combat boots

Baseball cap
Baseball pants
Green fatigue shirt
Baseball shoes (black)
Grey socks
Red and white socks
Green t-shirt (2)
Green boxer shorts
Green belt w/ brass buckle
Set of "dog" tags
Baseball shirt

Pfc. MELVIN PETERSON
Green fatigue pants
Green fatigue shirt
Green cap
Black combat boots
Baseball pants
Bastball shirt
Baseball cap
Grey socks
red and white socks
Green T-shirt (2)
Green boxer shorts
Green belt w/ brass buckle
Set of "dog" tags

PRIVATE SMALLS
Green fatigue pants
Green fatigue shirt
Black combat boots
Baseball cap (navy)
Baseball pants
Baseball shirt
Grey socks
Red and white socks

Green T-shirt (2)
Green boxer shorts
Green belt w/ brass buckle
Set of "dog" tags

PRIVATE C.J. MEMPHIS
    Green fatigue pants
    Green fatigue shirt
    Black combat boots
    Baseball cap (navy)
    Baseball pants
    Baseball shoes
    Grey socks
    Red and white socks
    Green T-shirt (2)
    Green boxer shorts
    Green belt w/ brass buckle
    Set of "dog" tags

LT. BYRD
    Green fatigue pants
    Green fatigue shirt
    Green fatigue cap
    Black combat boots
    Full dress uniform
    Black shoes
    Black socks
    Green T-shirt
    Set of "dog" tags
    MEDALS
    Army Good Conduct
    U.S.C.C. Expert Rifleman
    Two Bars, U.S. Cross Rifle

CAPT. WILCOX
    Green fatigue pants
    Green fatigue shirt

Green fatigue cap
Black combat boots
Full dress uniform
Black shoes
Black socks
Green T-shirt
Set of "dog" tags
MEDALS
Two Bars, U.S. Medical

CORPORAL ELLIS
Khaki shirt
Khaki pants
Khaki "cunt" cap
Black shoes
Black socks

PRIVATE HENSON
Green fatigue pants
Green shirt
Green fatigue cap
Black combat boots
Baseball pants
Baseball shirt
Baseball cap
Baseball shoes
Grey socks
Red and white socks
Green T-shirt (2)
Khaki shirt
Khaki pants
Khaki "cunt" cap

PRIVATE WILKIE
Green fatigue pants
Green fatigue shirt
Black combat boots

Baseball cap
Baseball pants
Baseball shoes
Red and white socks
Green T-shirt (2)
Khaki shirt
Khaki pants
Khaki "cunt" cap
Green fatigue cap

CAPTAIN DAVENPORT
Full dress uniform
Hat
Black shoes
Black socks
MEDALS
Two Bars, U.S. Judges A.
Army Good Conduct
Army Commission

COSTUME PLOT

ACT ONE

PRESET: ON STAGE

UP CENTER BOX (inside)
PETERSON
  Green fatigue hat
  Green fatigue shirt
UP STAGE LEFT BOX (inside)
COBB
  Green fatigue shirt
STAGE LEFT BOX (inside)
HENSON
  Green fatigue hat
  Green fatigue shirt

PRESET: BACK STAGE

BACK STAGE RIGHT
WILKIE
  Baseball pants
  Baseball shirt
  Baseball shoes
  Green fatigue hat
  Red and white socks
BACK STAGE CENTER
MEMPHIS
  Baseball pants
  Baseball shirt
  Baseball shoes

Baseball cap
Red and white socks
BACK STAGE LEFT
SGT. WATERS
   Green fatigue pants
   Green fatigue shirt
   Combat boots
   Dress uniform jacket
   Dress uniform "cunt" cap
   Helmet
PETERSON
   Baseball pants
   Baseball shirt
   Baseball shoes
   Baseball cap
   Red and white socks

ACT ONE

SERGEANT WATERS
   Full dress uniform (filthy)
   Black shoes
   Black socks
CAPTAIN TAYLOR
   Dress shirt
   Dress pants
   "Cunt" cap
   Black shoes
   Black socks
SMALLS
   T-shirt
   Fatigues
   Combat boots
   Grey socks

Green belt w/ brass buckle
Set of "dog" tags
CORPORAL ELLIS
Khaki shirt
Khaki pants
Black shoes
Black socks
"Cunt" cap
Khaki belt w/ brass buckle
CORPORAL COBB
Green fatigue pants (bloused in boots)
Green T-shirt
Combat boots
Grey socks
Green belt w/ brass buckle
Set of "dog" tags
PRIVATE HENSON
Baseball shirt
Green fatigue pants (bloused in boots)
Green T-shirt
Combat boots
Gray socks
Green belt w/ brass buckle
Set of "dog" tags
P.F.C. PETERSON
Green fatigue pants (bloused in boots)
Green T-shirt
Green belt w/ brass buckle
Combat boots
Grey socks
Set of dog tags
PRIVATE C.J. MEMPHIS
Green fatigue pants (bloused in boots)
Green fatigue shirt
Green T-shirt

Combat boots
Grey socks
Set of dog tags
P.F.C. PETERSON
Same as before

ACT ONE

PRIVATE HENSON
Baseball shirt
Baseball pants
Baseball shoes
Baseball cap
Green T-shirt
Red and white socks
Dog tags
PRIVATE SMALLS
Baseball shirt
Baseball pants
Baseball shoes
Baseball cap
Green T-shirt
Red and white socks
Dog tags
PRIVATE C.J. MEMPHIS
Baseball shirt
Baseball pants
Baseball shoes
Baseball cap
Green T-shirt
Red and white socks
Dog tags
CORPORAL COBB
Baseball shirt
Baseball pants

    Baseball shoes
    Baseball cap
    Green T-shirt
    Red and white socks
    Dog tags
PRIVATE WILKIE
    Green fatigue pants (bloused in boots)
    Green fatigue shirt
    Combat boots
    Baseball cap
    Green T-shirt
    Green belt w/ brass buckle
    Grey socks
    Set of dog tags

ACT ONE

CAPTAIN DAVENPORT
    Full dress uniform
    Hat
    Black shoes
    Black socks
CAPTAIN TAYLOR
    Same as before
CORPORAL ELLIS
    Same as before
PRIVATE WILKIE
    Same as scene one
    Green fatigue cap
    No baseball cap
SGT. WATERS
    Green fatigue pants (bloused in boots)
    Green fatigue shirt
    Green belt w/ brass buckle

Combat boots
Helmit
(QUICK CHANGE into)
    Full Dress Uniform
    Black shoes
    Black socks
    "Cunt" cap
(QUICK CHANGE)
    Full Dress Uniform (without jacket)
    Black shoes
    Black socks
P.F.C. PETERSON
    Baseball pants
    Baseball shirt
    Baseball cap
    Baseball shoes
    Green T-shirt
    Red and white socks
    (QUICK CHANGE)
        (Same as before)
        Dog tags
SERGEANT WATERS
    Green fatigue pants (bloused in boots)
    Green fatigue shirt
    Combat boots
    Black socks
    Green fatigue cap
PRIVATE WILKIE
    Baseball pants
    Baseball shirt
    Baseball cap
    Baseball shoes
    Green T-shirt
    Red and white socks
    Dog tags

CAPTAIN TAYLOR
  Green fatigue pants (bloused in boots)
  Green fatigue shirt
  Combat boots
  Black socks
  Green fatigue hat

ACT ONE

CAPTAIN TAYLOR
  Dress shirt
  Dress pants
  Black shoes
  Black socks
CAPTAIN DAVENPORT
  No change

ACT ONE

LIEUTENANT BYRD
  Green fatigue pants (bloused in boots)
  Green fatigue shirt
  Green T-shirt
  Black socks
  Combat boots
  Dog tags
  Green fatigue cap
CAPTAIN WILCOX
  Green fatigue pants (bloused in boots)
  Green fatigue shirt
  Green T-shirt
  Black socks
  Combat boots
  Dog tags
  Green fatigue cap

SERGEANT WATERS
  Same as Act One—2.

ACT TWO

PRESET: ON STAGE

UP CENTER BOX (inside)
PVT. C.J. MEMPHIS
  Green fatigue pants (folded)
  Combat boots
UP STAGE LEFT CENTER BOX (inside)
PVT. SMALLS
  Green fatigue pants (folded)
  Green fatigue shirt (folded)
  Combat boots
UP STAGE LEFT BOX (inside)
CPL COBB
  Green fatigue pants (folded)
  Green fatigue shirt (folded)
  Combat boots

DOWN STAGE LEFT BOX (inside)
PFC. PETERSON
  Green fatigue pants (folded)
  Green fatigue shirt (folded)
  Green fatigue hat
  Combat boots

PRESET: BACK STAGE

BACK STAGE LEFT
SGT. WATERS
  Dress uniform jackets (one filthy, one good)

DOWN STAGE LEFT
(Pvt. COBB)
  Combat boots
(PFC. PETERSON)
  Combat boots

ACT TWO

CAPTAIN DAVENPORT
  Same as ACT ONE

ACT TWO

PRIVATE HENSON
  Khaki pants
  Khaki shirt
  Khaki "cunt" cap
  Combat boots
  Dog tags

ACT TWO

PRIVATE SMALLS
  Green T-shirt
  Green boxer shorts
  Grey socks
  Dog tags
PRIVATE COBB
  Green T-shirt
  Green boxer shorts
  Grey socks
  Dog tags
PFC. PETERSON
  Green T-shirt
  Green boxer shorts

    Grey socks
    Dog tags
PVT. C.J. MEMPHIS
    Green T-shirt
    Green boxer shorts
    Dog tags
    No socks
SGT. WATERS
    Full dress uniform
    Black shoes
    Black socks
    Khaki "cunt" cap
PRIVATE WILKIE
    Khaki pants
    Khaki shirt
    Khaki "cunt" cap
    Combat boots

ACT TWO

CPL. ELLIS
    Same as before
CORPORAL COBB
    Green fatigue pants
    Green fatigue shirt
    Combat boots

ACT TWO

PRIVATE C.J. MEMPHIS
    Green fatigue pants (bloused in boots)
    Green fatigue T-shirt
    Combat boots

ACT TWO

SGT. WATERS
  Full dress uniform
  Khaki "cunt" cap
  Black shoes
  Black hat

ACT TWO

CAPTAIN TAYLOR
  Dress pants
  Dress shirt w/ tie
  Black shoes
  Black socks

ACT TWO

LT. BYRD
  Full dress uniform
  Black shoes
  Black socks
  Khaki "cunt" cap
CAPTAIN WILCOX
  Full dress uniform
  Black shoes
  Black socks
  Khaki "cunt" cap
CAPTAIN DAVENPORT
  No change
CAPTAIN TAYLOR
  No change

ACT TWO

CPL ELLIS
  No change

ACT TWO

PVT. WILKIE
  Green fatigue pants (bloused in boots)
  Green fatigue shirt
  Green fatigue cap
  Combat boots

ACT TWO

SGT. WATERS
  Dress pants
  Dress shirt w/ shirt
  Black shoes
  Black socks
PVT. C.J. MEMPHIS
  Green fatigue pants (bloused in boots)
  Green fatigue T-shirt
  Combat boots
  Dog tags

ACT TWO

CPL. ELLIS
  No change
PVT. HENSON
  Khaki pants
  Khaki shirt w/ tie
  Khaki "cunt" cap
  Khaki belt w/ brass buckle
  Combat boots

ACT TWO

CPL. COBB
  No change

ACT TWO

PRIVATE SMALLS
   Green fatigue pants (bloused in boots)
   Green fatigue shirt
   Green T-shirt
   Green belt w/ brass buckle
   Combat boots
CAPTAIN DAVENPORT
   No change

ACT TWO

SGT. WATERS
   Full dress uniform (filthy one)
   Khaki "cunt" cap
   Black socks
   Black shoes
PFC. PETERSON
   Green fatigue pants (bloused in boots)
   Green fatigue shirt
   Green fatigue hat
   Green belt w/ brass buckle
   Combat boots

ACT TWO

CAPTAIN TAYLOR
   Full dress uniform
   Khaki hat
   Black shoes
   Black socks

PROPERTIES LIST

4 boxes	Cartouches a blanc de 9mm
1	.45 Pistol (practical)
2	.45 Pistols (dummy)
3	Holsters w/belts
2	Backpacks
1 pkg	Envelopes
1	Letter writing pad
	Pencils
	Folders
6 pair	Ear plugs
4	Harmonicas (D,G,C,B,)
1	Guitar
1	Black pouch on string
4	Baseball bats in a bag
2	Baseballs
3	Baseball gloves
1	Briefcase
1 pr.	Sunglasses
	Legal pads
1	Clipboard w/pad
	Army papers
	201 File
	Investigation folder
1	Class ring
2	Watches (round faced, square faced)
1	Pipe
	Tobacco
1	Pipe stoker
	Pipe cleaners
1	Wallet w/photo

1 deck	Playing cards
1 box	Matches
2 books	Matches
2	Cigars (long, short)
1	Newspaper
1 pr.	Eyeglasses
	Lucky Strikes cigarettes
1	Shoe brush
	Boots
1	Table
2	Chairs
1	Chair for C.J.
	Boxes

PROPERTY PRE-SETS

STAGE RIGHT PROP TABLE

Brief case
  Folder w/legal pad
  pencil (in holder)
Sunglasses w/case
Clipboard w/
  Army letterhead papers
  Memos on Army stationary
201 Army Personnel File
Investigation File
Ear plugs (2 pair)

STAGE LEFT PROP TABLE

Pipe
Tobacco
Stoker
Matches (3 boxes)
Pipe cleaners
Deck of cards
Short cigar
Long cigar
Newspaper
pistol in holster
2 back packs
2 holsters
2 pistols
2 belts
pack Lucky Strikes

Guitar w/pic
5 Harmonicas
Ear plugs (2 pair)

DOWN LEFT PROP TABLE

Cloth sack w/4 baseball bats

DRESSING ROOMS
   Taylor
      Class ring
      Watch (round face)
   WATERS
      Wallet w/picture
      Watch (square face)
   PETERSON
      Eyeglasses w/case

ON STAGE

   ULC BOX
      Letter
      Writing pad
      Pencil
      Pack of envelopes
   UL BOX (inside)
      Shoe brush
   UR (over Box)
      Table
   SR Right of Platforms
      2 Chairs (stacked)

PROPS SCENE CHANGE
(End of Act I)

STRIKE

URC Large box (Smalls' bunk)
Small box LC
Bats from UC bunk
Baseball gloves
Boots from UL box (preset them SL prop table)

PLACE

Table flush to USR platform
Chairs under table
Small box URC
Preset C.J.'s chair for prison scene in SL-2
.45 pistol (for Wilkie) Dummy off SL
Clear shells from .45 practical and reload for Peterson

ACT 1 ONSTAGE PRESET POSITIONS: BOXES, COSTUMES AND PROPS

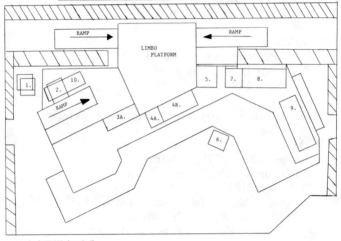

1. 2 CHAIRS (stacked)

2. TABLE and STAGE RIGHT BOX (table legs straddle the box)

3A. STAGE RIGHT CENTER BOX (large) (hinged)

4A. UP CENTER BOX (4B. hinged)
4B.   Green fatigue hat (PETERSON)
      Green fatigue Shirt

8. UP LEFT BOX (FAR LEFT)

9. STAGE LEFT BOX (hinged)
    Green fatigue (HENSON)
    Green fatigue hat

5. UP LEFT CENTER BOX (hinged)
    Letter Writing Pad Pencil
    Pack of envelopes

10. UPSTAGE RIGHT BOX (FAR RIGHT)

6. LEFT CENTER BOX

N.B: All the boxes function as bunks, footlockers, tsbles or chairs--depending
upon how they are used by the actors,
Boxes are placed w/hinges toward center.

7. UP STAGE LEFT BOX (hinged)
    Green fatigue hat (COBB)
    Green fatigue shirt
    Shoes brush
    Combat Boots

116

ACT 1P.10: Position of Boxes, Table and Chairs (as ELLIS places them)

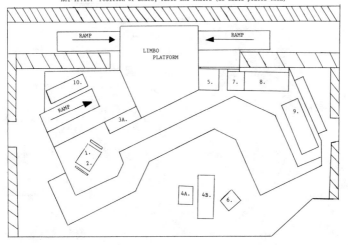

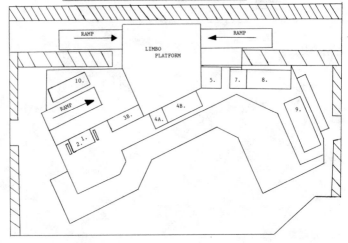

1. 2 CHAIRS (under table)

2. TABLE (parallel w/ platform)

3B. STAGE RIGHT CENTER BOX (hinged)
    (smaller length than Box 3A.)

4A. UP CENTER BOX

4B. Green fatigue pants (Pvt. C.J. MEMPHIS)
    Combat boots

5. UPSTAGE LEFT CENTER BOX (inside)
    Green fatigue pants shirt
    Combat boots

7. UPSTAGE LEFT BOX
    Green fatigue pants (Cpl. COBB)
    Green fatigue shirt

9. DOWN STAGE LEFT BOX (Pfc. PETERSON)
    Green fatigue pants
    Green fatigue shirt
    Green fatigue hat

118

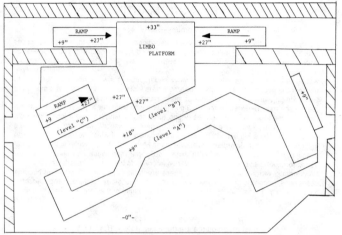

(SCALE: ½= 1'-0")

Other Publications for Your Interest

TALKING WITH . . .
(LITTLE THEATRE)
By JANE MARTIN

11 women—Bare stage

Here, at last, is the collection of eleven extraordinary monologues for eleven actresses which had them on their feet cheering at the famed Actors Theatre of Louisville—audiences, critics and, yes, even jaded theatre professionals. The mysteriously pseudonymous Jane Martin is truly a "find", a new writer with a wonderfully idiosyncratic style, whose characters alternately amuse, move and frighten us always, however, speaking to us from the depths of their souls. The characters include a baton twirler who has found God through twirling; a fundamentalist snake handler, an ex-rodeo rider crowded out of the life she has cherished by men in 3-piece suits who want her to dress up "like Minnie damn Mouse in a tutu"; an actress willing to go to any length to get a job; and an old woman who claims she once saw a man with "cerebral walrus" walk into a McDonald's and be healed by a Big Mac. "Eleven female monologues, of which half a dozen verge on brilliance."—London Guardian. "Whoever (Jane Martin) is, she's a writer with an original imagination."—Village Voice. "With Jane Martin, the monologue has taken on a new poetic form, intensive in its method and revelatory in its impact."—Philadelphia Inquirer. "A dramatist with an original voice . . . (these are) tales about enthusiasms that become obsessions, eccentric confessionals that levitate with religious symbolism and gladsome humor."—N.Y. Times. *Talking With* . . . is the 1982 winner of the American Theatre Critics Association Award for Best Regional Play.   (#22009)

(Royalty, $60–$40.
If individual monologues are done separately: Royalty, $15–$10.)

HAROLD AND MAUDE
(ADVANCED GROUPS—COMEDY)
By COLIN HIGGINS

9 men, 8 women—Various settings

Yes: *the Harold and Maude!* This is a stage adaptation of the wonderful movie about the suicidal 19 year-old boy who finally learns how to truly *live* when he meets up with that delightfully whacky octogenarian, Maude. Harold is the proverbial Poor Little Rich Kid. His alienation has caused him to attempt suicide several times, though these attempts are more cries for attention than actual attempts. His peculiar attachment to Maude, whom he meets at a funeral (a mutual passion), is what saves him—and what captivates us. This new stage version, a hit in France directed by the internationally-renowned Jean-Louis Barrault, will certainly delight both afficionados of the film and new-comers to the story. "Offbeat upbeat comedy."—Christian Science Monitor.   (#10032)

(Royalty, $60–$40.)

Plays FOR

BLACK CASTS and
BLACK and WHITE CASTS

AMEN CORNER

BLACKS, The

BLOOD KNOT

BLUES FOR MR. CHARLIE

CEREMONIES IN DARK OLD MEN

DUTCHMAN

GOLDEN BOY

GREAT WHITE HOPE, The

IN ABRAHAM'S BOSOM

IN WHITE AMERICA

MOON ON A RAINBOW SHAWL

MY SWEET CHARLIE

NO PLACE TO BE SOMEBODY

PURLIE VICTORIOUS

RAISIN IN THE SUN

ROLL SWEET CHARIOT

SIGN IN SIDNEY BRUSTEIN'S WINDOW

SLAVE

TAKE A GIANT STEP

TO BE YOUNG, GIFTED AND BLACK

SAMUEL FRENCH, Inc.

25 West 45th St.
NEW YORK 10036

7623 Sunset Blvd.
HOLLYWOOD 90046

#43

Bible Herstory

PATRICIA MONTLEY

(May Double.) Satire.

18 females—Bare Stage

Bible Herstory, a one-act feminist satire in six scenes featuring an all-woman cast. In "Paradise Abandoned," Eve convinces God not to stifle Her creativity just because She made a mistake in creating Adam. In "Noah's Ark-itect," Noah's wife and daughter prepare for the flood and "inspire" Noah to build a boat. "The Sacrifice of Sarah" shows Abraham's wife working on a theatrical project to save a lazy Isaac's life. In "Miriam in Labor," Moses' sister bargains with Pharaoh's daughter for better working conditions. In "Queen Solomon and the Paternity Suit," her Majesty proposes to cut in half a philandering charioteer claimed by both wife and mistress. In "The Renunciation," Mary rejects the Angel Gabriella's offer of the saviorship of the world, but agrees to have a son.

(Royalty, $20-$15.)

Out of Our Father's House

Play with music. (All Groups.)

BASED ON EVE MERRIAM'S

Growing Up Female in America: Ten Lives

3 females play 6 roles
Musicians—1 Interior

Arranged for the stage by Paula Wagner, Jack Hofsiss and Eve Merriam. Music by Ruth Cawford Seeger adapted by Daniel Schrier. With additional music by Daniel Shrier and Marjorie Lipari.

Taken entirely from diaries, journals and letters of the characters portrayed. They are a schoolgirl—founder of the Women's Suffrage Movement, an astronomer, a labor organizer, a minister, a doctor and a woman coming out of the Jewish ghetto. They are watched as they grow up, marry and bear children. They do not covet men's jobs, but when they want careers they are ostracized. A very moving play seen through the words and eyes of 19th century American women.
Write for information about music.

(Royalty, $20-$15.)

Other Publications for Your Interest

SPELL #7

(BLACK THEATRE GROUPS—CHOREOPOEM)

By NTOZAKE SHANGE, music by BUTCH MORRIS and DAVID MURRAY

4 men, 5 women—Interior

Another striking "choreopoem" from the pen of the author of *For Colored Girls* . . .! This one is set in St. Louis, in a bar frequented by Black artists and musicians, and is yet another meditation on the irony of being Black in a White world. Shange has her artists bare their souls in soliloquies, many of them illustrated by in-the-mood dances. "Spell #7 is humanely upbeat. In the end, (it) proclaims inner self-respect as the essential quality of black pride and black identity."—Christian Science Monitor. "An extremely fine theatre piece."—N.Y. Daily News. "A most lovely and powerful work."—N.Y. Times.

(Royalty, $50–$35.)

FOR COLORED GIRLS WHO HAVE CONSIDERED SUICIDE/WHEN THE RAINBOW IS ENUF

(LITTLE THEATRE)

By NTOZAKE SHANGE

7 women—Bare stage

For Colored Girls . . . is a passionately feminist spellbinder, a fluidly staged collection of vivid narrative pieces, some in prose and some in free verse, performed by seven young black women. It is almost exclusively concerned with the cavalier and sometimes downright brutal treatment accorded black women by their men. The play also captures the inner feelings of today's black women and goes beyond that to achieve its own kind of universality. Though their performances are mainly solo, the girls are united in much the same way as the cast in "A Chorus Line"—sometimes they sing together and on occasion dance together. And they are always united in sorrow, spirit, pride and soul. ". . . a triumphant event . . . filled with humor . . . joyous and alive, affirmative in the face of despair, and pure theatre."—N.Y. Daily News. ". . . a poignant, gripping, angry and beautiful theatre work."—Time. ". . . bitingly alive . . . overwhelming in its emotional impact . . . tragic, funny, proud and compassionate. . . ."—Newsweek.

(Royalty, $50–$40.)

FAVORITE BROADWAY DRAMAS

from

SAMUEL FRENCH, INC.

ALL THE WAY HOME – THE AMEN CORNER –
AMERICAN BUFFALO – ANASTASIA – ANGEL
STREET – BECKET – THE BELLE OF AMHERST –
BUTLEY – COLD STORAGE – COME BACK, LITTLE
SHEBA – A DAY IN THE DEATH OF JOE EGG –
A DELICATE BALANCE – THE DESPERATE HOURS
– THE ELEPHANT MAN – EQUUS – FORTUNE AND
MEN'S EYES – A HATFUL OF RAIN – THE
HOMECOMING – J.B. – KENNEDY'S CHILDREN –
LOOK HOMEWARD, ANGEL – A MAN FOR ALL
SEASONS – THE MIRACLE WORKER – A MOON FOR
THE MISBEGOTTEN – NO PLACE TO BE SOMEBODY
– ONE FLEW OVER THE CUCKOO'S NEXT – OUR
TOWN – A RAISIN IN THE SUN – THE RIVER
NIGER – THE SHADOW BOX – SIX CHARACTERS
IN SEARCH OF AN AUTHOR – STICKS AND BONES –
THE SUBJECT WAS ROSES – TEA AND SYMPATHY –
THE VISIT – WINGS

For descriptions of all our plays, consult our Basic Catalogue of Plays – available FREE.

Other Publications for Your Interest

THE CAINE MUTINY COURT-MARTIAL
(ALL GROUPS—DRAMA)
By HERMAN WOUK

19 men (6 nonspeaking)—Curtained set, desks, chairs and
dark blue uniforms of the U.S. Navy.

"The Caine Mutiny," the Pulitzer Prize novel hailed by critics as "the best sea story" and "the best World War II novel," has been adapted by the author in a version which is superior to the novel "in the artfullness of its craftsmanship." (N.Y. Herald Tribune.) "Enormously exciting. It is the modern stage at its best," said the Daily News. "Magnificent theatre," said the Mirror and the Journal-American. It is the court-martial proceedings against a young upright lieutenant who relieved his captain of command in the midst of a harrowing typhoon on the grounds that the captain was psychopathic in the crisis, and was directing the ship and its crew to its destruction. The odds and naval tradition are against the lieutenant. But as the witnesses and experts, some serious, some unwittingly comic, cross the scene of the trial, the weakness in the character of the captain is slowly revealed in a devastating picture of disintegration. An ideal play for all groups.

(Royalty, $50–$25.)

MEDAL OF HONOR RAG
(LITTLE THEATRE—DRAMA)
By TOM COLE

3 men (2 white, 1 black)

In an army hospital two very dissimilar men confront one another in a verbal sparring match. One, a psychiatrist—the other, "D.J.", a black ex-serviceman and holder of the Congressional Medal of Honor; an "honor" of that hangs on him like an ironic albatross. They also share one common experience—and guilt—they are both survivors in which many others perished. The psychiatrist gradually draws out of D.J. all the guilt, horror and disgust which left him traumatized. Always on guard against "whitie" and his values, D.J. is gradually revealed as a sensitive, intelligent, man nearly destroyed by his Viet Nam experience. His barriers crumbling, D.J. turns on the psychiatrist, exposing the man behind the professional facade. Yet D.J. desperately hopes—and the psychiatrist believes—he can be helped. But before another interview takes place, D.J. goes AWOL—and to get money for unpaid bills—is killed in an attempted robbery. "Cole has handled explosive with great intelligence and rich human understanding . . . beautifully written . . ."—WWD.

(Royalty, $50–$35.)

Other Publications for Your Interest

THE ROYAL HUNT OF THE SUN

(ALL GROUPS—HISTORY)

By PETER SHAFFER

22 men, 2 women—Cyc, drops, inset

The expedition of the Spanish under Pizzaro to the land of the Incas told in dazzling spectacle and moral chiaroscuro. After general absolution for any crimes they may commit against the pagan Incas, the conquerors set forth upon the sea. The Inca god is a sun god, ruler of the riches and people of Peru, and thought to be immortal. But the Spaniards have come in conquest rather than in reverence. There is a misunderstanding, confusion, and a slaughter in which the Spaniards kill 3000 unarmed and take the sun god captive. The ransom is 9000 pounds of gold. The avaricious Spaniards mutiny, try the sun god in kangaroo court, and then garrot him. He does not revive, and the Incas behold their dead god. "High intelligence and bold, imaginative reach . . . It has elements of the masque (and) pageant, soaring passages that recall the stage to its lofty enterprise, and a theme of enduring significance."—N.Y. Times. "Greatest play of our generation."—London Daily Mail.

(Royalty, $50–$25.)

BLACK COMEDY

(LITTLE THEATRE—FARCE)

By PETER SHAFFER

5 men, 3 women—Interior

Taking a page from the Chinese theatre, this farce opens on a dark stage (which is light to the characters), then blows a fuse throwing them all in the dark (which is light to the audience), and ends with lights reconnected (i.e., with a dark stage). What we see in the "dark" is this: A girl bringing her wealthy father to meet her fiance, an improvident sculptor, and to impress him, the sculptor has both invited a wealthy art patron and stolen the fine furniture from the apartment next door for his bare pad. Not only have the lights gone out, but everything else turns cockeyed—the neighbor returns too soon, the art patron is mistaken for an electrician, and a former flame pixies the proceedings from the bedroom. "Grand slapstick . . . Jolted me with laughter, and I was sorry indeed when the stage went dark and farce ended."—N.Y. Daily News. "A remarkably ingenious farce."—Wall Street Journal. "A truly hilarious and original farce . . . facial situations and amusing characters that keep the hilarity spinning festively in the air."—N.Y. Post. "An evening with this uproarious play is like the rediscovery of laughter."—N.Y. World Journal Tribune. One of the biggest hits of the season and a perfect play for Little Theatre and College groups.

(Royalty, $50–$25.)

#W-7